KATIE ROIPHE

STILL

SHE

HAUNTS

ME

A NOVEL

DELTA TRADE PAPERBACKS

A Delta Book
Published by
Dell Publishing
a division of
Random House, Inc.
1540 Broadway
New York, New York 10036

Grateful acknowledgment is made to the following for permission to quote from previously unpublished material:

AP Watt Ltd on behalf of the Trustees of the C L Dodgson Estate.

Alfred C. Berol Collection, Fales Library, New York University.

Cover design and photo manipulation by Royce M. Becker
Cover photo © Jon Feingersh/The Stock Market

ISBN 0-385-33530-X

Reprinted by arrangement with The Dial Press

Manufactured in the United States of America

Published simultaneously in Canada

October 2002

10 9 8 7 6 5 4 3 2 1
BVG

For Harry

I am assured by Major Dodgson and Miss F. Menella Dodgson that in the very revealing matter discovered in his numerous diaries, there is not the slightest suggestion that he either felt or inspired any pangs of tender passion.

—LANGFORD REED, 1932
The Life of Lewis Carroll

We met a great many other interesting people, among them Lewis Carroll, author of the immortal *Alice*—but he was only interesting to look at, for he was the stillest and shyest full-grown man I have ever met. . . .

—MARK TWAIN

For some reason, we know not what, his childhood was sharply severed. It lodged in him whole and entire. He could not disperse it.

—VIRGINIA WOOLF,
"Lewis Carroll"
The Moment and Other Essays

STILL

SHE

HAUNTS

ME

The letter came by the afternoon post just as he was putting the finishing touches on his Euclid lecture. He tore open the envelope, took out a cream-colored page with scalloped edges, and saw the familiar script. He felt himself vanishing, skin, hair, mouth, until all that was left was a single point of pain.

It is no longer desirable for you to spend time with our family.

He left the letter on the hall table, folded like a closed door.

His eyes moved to the black albums that now took up three shelves of the bookcase that stretched to the ceiling. 1,031 photographs, each labeled in scratchy print on the bottom right-hand corner. His point of view made visible. The past sliced into stills. He reached for an album looking for the photographs of

Alice in the straw Chinaman's hat that tied under her chin; Alice pretending to be asleep on a fur throw outside; Alice sitting with her ankles crossed next to a fern. He had the sudden feeling he was looking into the window of someone else's house. He put the album back without opening it.

A dusty orange light floated in through the tall window. On the mahogany writing table were the diaries, fawn-colored leather scratched, spines broken, pages warped. He pulled out the fourth volume and flipped to the month of April. He took a straight razor out of the drawer and ran it down each offending page; it cut with a pleasing violence, slicing through the tiny cottony threads, neat but somehow fleshlike. A surgeon of himself.

As each sheet fell to the floor he felt lighter. The diaries will contain omissions. Unsaid passages, unspoken frames of mind. Missing bits of bones and cartilage.

Why should it matter? He never entirely understood the compulsion to record, his own or anyone else's. Why every trivial event had to be chatted about with one's conscience: exposed and not exposed. It was a tricky game, a diary. A completely and utterly private document that went to great lengths to explain itself to others.

While he hated the idea of anyone reading through the diaries, in any abbreviated or edited shape, in the near or distant future, the fact that he wrote them suggested otherwise. He was creating a sympathetic companion, a phantom thrown up by his own words, an illusion cut and formed out of vacant hours; the idea of someone who would, in spite of everything, slog through financial calculations and insomniac musings on the precise plum color of the sky. But that was the beauty of it—it was only the *idea* of someone.

So much of what he was writing was monotonous. So much of it boiled down to red potatoes for dinner alongside his mutton. The monotony itself may have been part of the point, of course, the soothing patter that fell like drizzle on the window of the old library at night; the routine scratched in steel nub on soft paper, running down the page in India brown. Every entry breathed boredom. What was the diary but a demonstration of how banal his life was, how ordinary, how like everyone else's life, certain starts and skips excluded, it really was? It reassured him, writing each page, that there was nothing interesting there.

Uneven patches of heat floated mysteriously through his rooms, several conflicting weather climates at once, but he could feel the draft on his shoulders. He sipped his tea which was now cold.

It is no longer desirable for you to spend time with our family.

He had first met Alice seven years earlier. Late afternoon, April 25, 1856. He had just been appointed to the prestigious position of mathematical lecturer at Christ Church, Oxford, after five years as a student there. This was in addition to his slightly less prestigious position as sublibrarian, which paid thirty-five pounds a year. He was twenty-four years old and solely responsible for the mathematical elucidation of 180 undergraduates. He lived on the second floor of the old library of Christ Church. And his furniture, what little of it there was—two tufted armchairs, a globe on a brass stand, two telescopes, a purple Turkish carpet, a faded red satin divan embroidered with an oriental flower pattern, an old square writing table— was dwarfed by his new surroundings. There was the black marble mantel over the fireplace, the curling wrought-iron chandelier that hung high in the center of the room, and the view of creamy apple blossoms through the window. He still hadn't entirely settled in. There were piles of books on the floor and calculations and diagrams for his paper in progress, "The Fifth Book of Euclid Proved Algebraically," strewn everywhere.

The Christ Church library was across the green from the deanery, a long magnificent building covered in ivy, with crenellated towers, tall mullioned windows, and an arched doorway. He had met the new dean, a large handsome man with thinning hair and an aquiline nose that placed him firmly in the classical period he studied. And he had seen his wife from a distance. A dark-haired woman in a flapping straw hat bent over tulips. But he had not yet met the children.

He continued to cut pages from the diary. *The photographs of the cathedral did not turn out well.* Arcs of white paper gathered by his feet, catching the light like the bows of small white boats.

He thought of *A Midsummer Night's Dream,* which he had gone over and over with his speech therapist, until the lines dissolved into sounds. There, center stage, was Titania in love with a donkey. A few drops of liquor, a juice squeezed from a purple flower called "love-in-idleness," has put the fairy queen under a spell. *What thou seest when thou dost wake, Do it for thy truelove take; Love and languish for his sake.* After she wreathes the donkey in fragrant flowers, the spell is lifted. But there is a moment in the play, not in it exactly but implied by it; the moment when she opens her eyes and sees the stiff gray bristle of donkey flank, before she has fallen out of love. Still enspelled, but suddenly aware. The moment Titania observes, as if from a balcony, with a binocular, her own desire. *Swift as a shadow, short as any dream . . . The jaws of darkness do devour it up. So quick bright things come to confusion.* To see that impossible love laid out in front of you and still be caught in it, that lonely time, not released but trapped. All the beauty and ugliness you are capable of converging in this one love—that part of *A Midsummer Night's Dream* was as true and accurate as any photograph Dodgson had ever taken. The heart's rough quiet. Donkeys running wild.

I

The sky was yellow gray that first day. Drifting past them were ragged dark clouds with bright burning edges. Dodgson and an old friend, Reginald Southey, were carrying their cameras and equipment to the cathedral. Southey had long hair tucked behind his ears and the swarthy coloring of a sailor, even though he was studying to be a physician. Dodgson had recently photographed him with his arm draped around the shoulder of a skeleton, to capture his good-natured morbidity. The casual, friendly approach medical men took toward death.

The two men carried with them the portable dark tent with its yellow calico curtain, a tripod, bottles, trays, glass measures and funnels. Dodgson had just bought his camera for fifteen pounds a month earlier, from T. Ottiwell of Charlotte Street, and it was still heavy and awkward in his hands.

The afternoon light was silvery, the tower of the cathedral dulled by glowing fog. It would lift though, Dodgson was fairly sure as he looked up at the sky. He began unpacking the heavy metal tripod, setting up the tent that would serve as a makeshift darkroom, uncorking the brown bottle of collodion, and pouring the strong-smelling nitrate solution into a tray. The two men began framing photographs. Formal landscapes were what they were after, stiffly posed portraits of building and sky.

Dodgson loved the spires and towers of the university, the overlapping grays, the chipped and mottled stone over green sprays of wild grass. He loved the large, circular pool in the middle of Tom Quad, the round symmetrical sensibleness of it, black water reflecting broken cloud. Christ Church felt like a fortress to him, peaceful and protected and entirely isolated. Time moved differently here; it hovered and clung.

Still, the new dean was intent on changing the physical face of the university, stripping the dark oak paneling from inside the cathedral, for instance. But unlike most of the other young lecturers, Dodgson resisted. He liked the ancient, unchangeable solidity, the perpetually disintegrating aspect of the place that somehow hinted at the impossibility of it ever truly falling apart. He liked the arched doorways and low-ceilinged halls, the loom and coolness at once churchy and castlelike.

Dodgson put his camera down. His hands were sticky from collodion. He wiped them with a cloth he had tucked into his pocket, and brought the camera back to his face.

Everything that flickered could be made permanent. That was what drew him to photography, what made every painstaking step worth it: the permanence of the image. That was what fascinated him, the working against time; the black art, it was called, which did have the power to stop the visual progression, the disintegration of the moment into a worse one—the bird that would fly off the branch.

He and Southey stood on the edge of the deanery lawn. Through the rosewood camera he could see the sun slowly burning through the fog. Then a patch of blue. The cathedral shadowed in triangles, hexagons, and rectangles. He aimed at the cathedral, cutting off the tiny fluttering leaves in order to include the spire and then cutting off the spire in order to frame the building with tiny fluttering leaves, and then stumbling backward holding the camera. He loved the precision, the small slice of shadow under each leaf, that came across in photographs, in perfect, almost scientific detail.

Southey was off to the side concentrating on the garden.

"Have a look," he said, stepping back for Dodgson to see.

There through the viewfinder in the deanery garden was a tall dark-haired woman in a chocolate brown dress, which was billowing slightly in the wind.

They moved closer. Dodgson took her in through the lens, black hair pulled back from her face in scalloped waves, pale, luminous skin, fine lines fanning out around her eyes, not detracting at all from her prettiness but instead giving sadness and depth to her strange, sharply angled face, which had the odd dimensional perspective of a Renaissance portrait. Her most striking feature by far was her mouth, her large pillowy lips. They saved her face from looking cool. There was no doubt that she was beautiful.

"There is a likeness I should not mind taking," Southey said.

The woman turned toward the two young men on the edge of her lawn and waved.

"Won't you come and have ginger beer with us?" she called out.

"It would be our pleasure," called Southey.

She seemed barely old enough to be the wife of the dean, barely thirty, if that.

Behind her were three girls, dark and pretty like their mother, playing croquet. Or rather the two oldest were playing croquet and the youngest, who could not have been more than two, was tilting unsteadily toward the wickets and grabbing them. A pear-shaped woman with yellow hair was standing in the shade. She must be the nurse, Dodgson thought.

He watched the youngest careen. Amazing how oblivious children are to their own bodies. He watched her fall.

"I'm Reginald Southey," said Southey.

Dodgson stood there. He felt a familiar wave of panic.

"And this is Charles Dodgson."

"You must be the new mathematical lecturer," she said, smiling. "We have so wanted to make your acquaintance."

"Yes, I have seen you before, but . . ." He flushed. "I was hoping to meet you. The whole family."

"And I hope you have come with the express intention of taking our likenesses," she said.

"N-n-nothing would make me happier."

"These are my daughters," she said, gesturing toward the girls. "Lorina, Alice, Edith."

Dodgson turned toward the girls. Southey barely glanced at them. Like most men his age Southey had a studied indifference to children, which was meant to point out his independence and enhance his virility. But Dodgson had always liked children. Or as he once put it in a letter to a friend, "I'm fond of children (except boys)."

"So you are studying medicine," Mrs. Liddell was saying to Southey.

"Yes, dabbling with skeletons."

Dodgson shaded his eyes so he could see better. The girls were running across the lawn, batting the ball, their skirts flying behind them.

His eye was drawn to the middle one. Alice. The least pretty. Not an inanimate doll-beauty like the others, but a dark, wild, tousled thing. Her legs and arms too long, sunbrowned, her hair short for a girl, almost boyish, and messy, sticking up, as if she had just woken up, the front cut unevenly; no doubt she squirmed under the scissors. Her face was pointed. Her eyes enormous and complicated and black.

And then there was the slightest trace of theater in her stance. She ran a little too fast. She concentrated a little too intently on the ball. She swung a little too hard when she hit it. All of which served to make her more *there* than her sisters.

The oldest, Lorina, fished under a hedge for the ball. Alice turned to stare in a way he had never seen a child stare. The darkness of her eyes and arch of her eyebrows gave her an expression of cool skepticism entirely incongruous in someone her age.

"Isn't it awful, all of that sawing living creatures apart?" Mrs. Liddell was saying.

"I am afraid most of us actually enjoy it," Southey said.

Alice was oddly foreign-looking for the middle of Oxford. Next to her sisters, ordinary, British, pale-skinned, ruddy-cheeked, well-fed, it was striking how different she looked. The other two were like paler versions of her, white where Alice was nut-colored, soft and round where Alice was sharp. If they were photographs, they would be blurred, overexposed versions of their more radiant sister. Or so it seemed to Dodgson.

Mrs. Liddell patted back a stray curl that had blown loose in the wind. She looked out at the game. Dodgson saw a slight tightening of her smile when her eyes rested on her middle daughter, a watchfulness that did not descend on the other two.

"Do have some ginger beer," Mrs. Liddell said, pouring two glasses.

The men, one short, one tall, were standing with her mother against the lime-colored grass. The sun was in her eyes. Shimmering diamonds between leaves. White dots on the inside of her eyelids when she blinked. She could feel the men watching her. She stuck out her stomach.

A blue ball spun hard into the arch of Dodgson's foot.

He looked down and moved his shoe.

"I'm sorry," Alice said, running up to him. "But I believe it's your turn."

She held up the mallet with both hands.

He stooped to take it.

"This is the new mathematical lecturer, Alice," said Mrs. Liddell.

"Are you going to lecture me?"

Mrs. Liddell watched Dodgson wander off into the game with her poised and disheveled middle daughter, whose bow, she noticed, was lopsided and coming untied. He seemed shy, standing there without saying anything for so long, taking in a child's croquet game like it was the ceiling of the Sistine Chapel.

She watched her four-year-old daughter running through the lawn, her hair blue-black in the sun, pulling the tall young man by the hand.

While Lorina Liddell often furnished her children's futures, down to the addresses in London, wallpaper, and china patterns, she had trouble with Alice. She couldn't imagine how her unruly daughter was going to fit into the exalted society she had always planned for her children, the dinner tables packed with dukes and ladies and famous novelists and cabinet members.

Her own insecurities clustered around the single issue of social origin. William Thackeray, who was a classmate of Henry Liddell, wrote to a mutual friend when the Liddells married: "Dear brave old Liddell . . . has taken a 3rd rate provincial lady (rather first rate in the beauty line, though, I think) for a wife. . . ." Though the nineteen-year-old Lorina Hannah Liddell could not have known about this remark, she woke up the morning after her wedding with the uneasy feeling that this exact sentiment was being discussed over breakfast by remote acquaintances. After all, the dean's mother's uncle was the brother of the eighth earl of Strathmore, and his father's father was a baronet. The new Mrs. Liddell worried that in spite of her cashmere burnoose with tassels and sable-trimmed pelisse and her blue satin with lace and rose-trimmed flounces, her 3rd rate provincialism showed.

Is your family having a portrait painted? their Oxford friend Mrs. Lamb once asked Alice. *You look so unusually neat.* Mrs. Liddell couldn't hide her annoyance when the comment was repeated to her. But she couldn't deny that Alice was perpetually in disarray. Once there was a mat in the back of her hair so daunting, so difficult to untangle, that they were forced to cut out a hunk of it, which made the thin bristling remainder in the back of her neck impossible to smooth down. She was embarrassed that her middle daughter should seem so uncared for, even though she lived in a perfectly ordered house, even though both of her sisters managed to keep perfectly reasonable heads of hair. They had long ago given up trying to get her hair to hold any sort of curl. It was soft and fine and straight, not at all the sort of hair that should be difficult to care for, and yet it was. Which only made it worse that her clothes were often stained, wrinkled, crumpled, or undone, shedding buttons, trailing sashes, losing hems. Or that mysterious bruises were constantly emerging, in yellows and purples, on her arms and legs. There was no reason, no tangible moment when her appearance started unraveling; it just happened naturally when she stepped out of the house to play for five minutes, or even if she didn't. Mrs. Liddell was endlessly bothered by her middle daughter's dishevelment, but there was nothing she could do, no amount of vigilance, no amount of forcing her to stay still, that would stop the inevitable progression of disorder.

Dodgson stepped carefully over a wicket with Alice's hand in his. A man and a girl. A man and his idea of a girl. Lifted out of poems like Wordsworth's "We Are Seven." The poet writes about a curly-haired eight-year-old who insists that there are seven children in her family even though two of them are dead. She doesn't understand that death has made them five. That is the girl Dodgson was looking for. The girl of his dreams. She takes her supper out to her brother's and sister's graves and sits crosslegged in the grass, not out of innocence exactly, but a kind of stubbornness. *The first that died was sister Jane; In bed she moaning lay.* The poem has a frantic undercurrent, barely suppressed and contained. *Till God released her of her pain; And then she went away.* She knows. She doesn't want to know. The result is a kind of play, but it is more than play, it is an overturning of death, an ability to sit and eat your dinner over it, because the mind is that strong and flexible. Seven minus two is not five. The fierceness of imagination required to produce that thought is what Dodgson found so charming in little girls. That is what it meant to him, the old romantic saw that children are close to God, that the dust of creation is still on them. That is what innocence is, the word that dances and eludes: it is the refusal of death.

Dodgson felt the wind in his face as he walked next to Alice. He felt hope opening up over the expanse of croquet wickets. Like a picnic over graves.

2

$\mathbf{D}$odgson had gotten into trouble three sentences into his symbolic-logic lecture. He stood in the front of the room, the students scattered between empty chairs, outlining the tantalizing pleasures of symbolic logic in front of the chalkboard, when it happened.

He was in the middle of saying: "The universe contains things, for example, 'I' 'London,' 'roses,' and these things have attributes, for example 'large,' 'red,' 'old.' Throwing these things and attributes in relation to each other is the basis of symbolic logic, without which I assure you we cannot live our—"

While he faltered, time cracked apart and slowed. "L-l-l-l." He could feel it on the roof of his mouth, the patting of his tongue. The balance of power tilted, inviting his students in to mock him, making even the dullest feel superior. And yet, they were good about it. They shifted in their seats; they took suddenly copious notes, rustled purposefully through papers. He could feel their generosity, their discomfort on his behalf filling the room like sunlight. But the old mortification shot through him.

He finally got it out. *Lives*. But he had lost the attention of the class. Their concentration was invisible, but when you were teaching you could feel it, dense and forceful like the wind. And when you lost it you could feel it too, the lack of tautness and direction in the air.

At home, at the tiny brick parsonage at Daresbury, and then later at the large three-story Georgian rectory at Croft, no one cared about his stutter. He sat for hours on the floor of the nursery reciting poems and monologues and performing puppet plays for his sisters and brothers without noticing it. *T-t-t-time, my love, is flowing, And I fear I must be going*. He glided over it like the iced-over pond behind the rectory.

But when he got to Rugby the boys followed him around the grassless courtyard, calling him "D-d-d-dodo." That became his name, Dodo. After a bird that had been extinct since 1681. A bird that was hunted and killed by Dutch sailors and colonists on a remote island in the Indian Ocean. One of the earliest known species destroyed by men. They were awkward-looking things, dodo birds, all stomach and bill.

One afternoon he came back after a Latin lesson to find everything upside down, books, trousers, bed, inkpot, candle, even the red geraniums his sister Elizabeth had sent were somehow balanced on their blooms. Later he recognized the imagination and humor that had gone into the gesture, but at the time it was simply an effective means of communication:

He was skewed. When he opened the door he was ashamed, as if something in him had been laid bare.

And his stutter got worse, particularly his b's, d's, and l's; it got so bad that he would drag his pen along the grooves in his desk, like dark rivers, pretending not to know the answers in class so he wouldn't have to speak. He turned himself into that strangest of paradoxes, the boy who reads all the time, does brilliantly on tests, but is stupid in class. Outside it was harder. He ate his dinner at the end of the last bench in the dining hall, his head bowed down in exaggerated interest in the potatoes bobbing in the salty stew so that no one would think he minded being left out of the conversation. He learned shyness at school, mastering it more thoroughly than Latin or geometry.

When he came home for winter holidays during his second year barely able to get through a sentence without chopping it up, his father decided to take him to a specialist, Dr. Bradshaw, the next town over. The doctor sat behind his desk as Dodgson's father explained the problem at great and painful length, and then both men looked expectantly at him. Dodgson sat on the salmon-colored sofa. Perversely, he couldn't stutter. The words flew out whole, his speech suddenly fluid and eloquent in a way it hadn't been in years. His father looked at him, betrayed. But Dr. Bradshaw took his father's word for it, and soon his fingers were circling the boy's neck so tightly he thought they would leave fingerprints.

"We shall have your voice smooth as silk," he purred. Then he proceeded to place an uncomfortable, medieval-looking metal contraption in Dodgson's throat. He was supposed to keep it there an hour a day to "ease the passageway." After several weeks Dodgson was left parched and swollen and stuttering worse than ever.

And then, at Oxford, the situation improved. Stuttering was a sign of erudition, a donnish quirk. No longer freakish. But still it sometimes overtakes and confounds him, finding its way into his speech at an awkward moment, bringing back small figures darting through a mud stone courtyard. He could feel people saying it: Quite a queer fish, that Dodgson.

His most recent consultation was with an Edinburgh phrenologist, Mr. Hamilton. After feeling his head with soft, sausage-shaped fingers, Hamilton wrote, "The great activity and volatile action of your mind is caused by the mixed sanguine nervous temperament." While Dodgson had been interested in his report, and in the tangential information, "you could have been a medical man," he could not honestly say it had helped.

He knew it was pointless to try to do anything about the stutter. All of the specialists in the kingdom couldn't give him the basic fluency of a five-year-old child. Yet every now and then he thought of going to see Dr. James Hunt, the renowned author of *A Manual of the Philosophy of Voice and Speech, Especially in Relation to the English Language and the Art of Public Speaking*. He'd heard that Hunt had considerable success with several of the students. And when he was seated next to Hunt at a breakfast in the Common Room, the doctor had invited him to come to see him at his house near Oxford.

Dodgson knew that even without the stutter he was not a gifted teacher. He had made his peace with that bit of information in the first weeks of his lectureship. He had trouble sympathizing with minds that could not keep up with his, trouble keeping the condescension out of his tone. How could anyone have difficulty with parallelograms?

Many of his students were simply not prepared. Prestigious places like Eton thrust them into universities with an appalling ignorance of basic mathematical principle. They could easily slip through even the best schools, fluent in Greek but not knowing what a hypotenuse was. And a large number of them would fail no matter how brilliantly he tutored. At first this was a subject of scandal to him, but lately it had become a relief. He did not have to take their ignorance personally.

But he did find it frustrating to watch these aristocrats dabble and to feel part of their dabbling. To be a don of dabbling. The thing that fascinated Dodgson most was how at ease they were in the world. Several mornings ago, he came across one young lord, rumpled, fully dressed in a midnight-blue velvet coat and satin scarf, asleep in the shrubbery, where he had evidently collapsed the night before. He looked up dreamily, rubbed the leaves and grass out of his blond hair, and said, "Well, hullo, Mr. Dodgson. Beautiful day," before wandering off in the direction of his room. Dodgson couldn't get over the good-natured, unfazed look in his bloodshot eyes.

Most of them seemed to find their bewilderment in the face of knowledge and tradition charming. Graceful, arrogant boys who wore their lack of comprehension like a gardenia in their buttonholes. They slept through most of their lectures. On weekends, they slipped into town and met garish women. They wore close-cut breeches and sealskin waistcoats. They held champagne parties in their rooms that lasted all night. They all seemed to keep dogs too, as if they had wandered into Christ Church from a giant hunting party. They were not here to learn, these curled darlings of the British empire; they were here so that during whiskey- and smoke-filled lunches in their clubs twenty years hence these ex-beautiful boys, now balding, with large stomachs, could utter the words, *Back at Oxford . . .*

As Dodgson walked diagonally toward his rooms, his notes tucked under his arm, he saw a hole that had been dug for a pipe. Improvements were being made. He stood at the edge of the hole, which was approximately the size of a dinner plate, and peered down the sides, the ripped surface glossy, almost black, bits of root sticking through, the dirt rough, shiny specks of mineral glittering in the sun. If he had not been looking he could have fallen in, he thought to himself, annoyed.

He looked down into the hole, the dark brown shading into black. He couldn't isolate the precise moment where it was too dark to see, only witnessed the tunneling, experienced the end of sight, the anxious straining of the eye. There was no bottom, only a looming blackness, and suddenly he felt his stomach lurching. The dark hole in the earth seemed to threaten, to gape and to yearn, but for what? The ten feet of pipe that was going to fill it? Metal. Progress. He was perfectly capable of stepping around it and walking confidently on to his rooms, but he didn't. He stood at its mouth, stuck and falling at the same time.

❧

Somehow Dodgson was most at home sitting in a boat, feeling the sensual resistance of water beneath oar. He had invited Mrs. Liddell, Lorina, Alice, and Edith out on a boat ride down an auxiliary of the Thames. They had gathered at Folly Bridge, the girls and their mother in large hats, the swans drifting past the dock. Picnics had always appealed to him, shaking everything up, taking everything out of its place, boiled eggs and little silver salt shakers on the grass, flower patterns on good china competing with ants, linen balanced on laps. The architecture of society falling away, the walls and doors and addresses that divide suddenly opening into air and sky and tree—everyone jumbled together under a canopy of leaves.

The wool blanket was spread out on the sloping riverbank. Dodgson lay on his side, propping himself up with his elbow. Alice was leaning against his legs, peeling an egg. Edith was sitting a little ways off pulling up grass from the dirt, and Miss Prickett was batting her arm to get her to stop. Mrs. Liddell was washing her hands in the river, and Ina was taking strawberries out of the large wicker basket and putting them on plates.

Time seemed slippery and unmanageable. He felt himself pulled back into childhood, sitting with his sisters, a great mass of petticoats floating up under their skirts, the girlish chatter swirling around his head, enveloping him like perfume. The daffodils outside Daresbury butter-yellow on the lawn, dipping their heads in the breeze, the girls playing with each other's hair, gossiping. He was meant to be inside doing his lessons, but he wanted nothing more than to float with his sisters, to be consumed by them. He was five years old but he was a man. His father's oldest son. Heir to his hunting and sermons, to the great deer head on the wall of the library that made him queasy every time he saw it. Head without neck. He didn't have the easy, confident assumption of authority that his father the reverend did: look at me, I have entered the room. He didn't have that. He melted. He slipped away. Wanting nothing more than to be left alone.

He spent hours in his room worrying about basic facets of life that other people glided over, like the afternoon he realized that time moved slower for him than for his seven-year-old sister, Elizabeth, because each minute that passed was a greater proportion of his life than hers. This thought nagged at him, made him anxious, since time was supposed to be the same for everyone, the absolute unit of measurement upon which everyone could agree, five minutes, a half hour, but it wasn't. Time bent and swayed depending on who you were.

A rock splashed in the water. Alice.

Lorina got up to scoop it out. Even outdoors, her instinct was to clean up after Alice. She also had a passion for rocks. Her drawers overflowed with them. A friend of the family had given her a battered, rose-colored copy of Louis Agassiz's *Recherches sur les poissons fossiles*, which she kept by her bed along with Charles Lyell's *Principles of Geology*.

On the way home, they drifted through the thickening fog, which made it impossible to see the wild grasses on the shore. A duck skimmed the water and splashed the boat. And then, as if the air could not hold the moisture, it started to drizzle just as the dock came into view.

On shore, Alice ran under Dodgson's coat, which he held over her head as they walked. The other two girls followed with their mother and nurse. To distract them from the rain, which was now coming down harder, he began telling a story. It was about an emu, a dodo, and a mouse who cried so much they created a pool of tears. They swam into a cave, worrying the whole time that they would drown. There they sat through a history lesson so boring it dried them out.

Alice was soaked, her hair plastered to her face, her white dress transparent, clinging. She was smiling, water dripping down her forehead, into her eyes, drops sticking to her lashes. She started running. "Catch me," she called, and he ran, both of them sprinting, it was amazing how fast Alice could run, and finally as they reached the gate he caught her, rain in his eyes, pulling her up, soaking and kicking her legs and screaming, "Put me down, Mr. Dodgson, put me down." He wouldn't have picked her up except for the rain, which created its own chaotic sideshow, its own holiday atmosphere. Mrs. Liddell caught up with them, with a sobbing Edith and Ina beside her, and he put Alice, still kicking, back on the ground, and the whole wet party pressed forward.

"What *imagination* you have, Mr. Dodgson," said Mrs. Liddell as he held the door to the deanery open for the girls.

But there was disapproval in her voice. She sees through him, Mrs. Liddell. For all of the featheriness of her existence, the pale blue silks swishing through reception rooms. For all of the frivolity, the parties spilling out onto her lawn, lit up for the occasion with lanterns, the tableaux vivants and ices after dinner, she understands. She sees that he is trying to escape. Trying to take what God has given us and twist it and undo it and put it backward. That his imagination, as she so disapprovingly refers to it, is a way of transporting himself out of any momentary melancholy. Of literally changing the world when he cannot bear it the way it is.

There was an echo, an unsettling familiarity in her words, *what imagination you have, Mr. Dodgson.* He could hear his father in those words. His father, who worried something was wrong from the moment his small son arranged the forty-nine pieces in the Life of Christ jigsaw puzzle so that the adult Jesus was holding the baby Jesus, and one of the wise men had a head of fishes. His father did not like when he started drawing cartoons of strange little people with wild snaking hair or when he began putting out the family newspaper, the Rectory Umbrella. He did not like the theater Dodgson built and painted for the nearly life-size shrivel-faced marionettes, or the way he moved his fingers in the strings to make the wooden figures nod and bow. He did not like his son's comic opera about the railway, *La Guida di Bragia by Mr. B. Webster.* The parts of Ebenezer Mooney and Julius Caesar Spooney and Mrs. Muddle were performed by his marionettes. *(Why may not marionettes be just as good, As larger actors made with flesh and blood?)* His father worried that with each dangle and lift of a marionette's head, the persona he had invented for his son's future, the Reverend Charles Lutwidge Dodgson, with a country parish, a pleasantly plump wife, and five children, was drifting out of reach. That solid, decent fellow would never sit at the head of a thick oak table and carve a ham. *(Oh, Spooney, Spooney, in the gravest and the saddest moments, how can you thus intrude your absurd remarks? Be sensible, Spooney!)* "Why do you need to turn everything on its head, Charles," he used to ask him, half annoyed and half wondering, "isn't the world beautiful and harmonious as it is?"

Several years later, when Dodgson finally earned his father's approval, it felt strange and coercive. After winning several academic awards at Oxford, he wrote crankily to his sister Elizabeth: "I am quite tired of being congratulated on various subjects: There seems no end to it. If I had shot the dean I could hardly have more said about it."

He had starred and underlined this stanza in his Moroccan leather edition of Andrew Marvell's verse:

The mind . . . creates, transcending these,
Far other worlds and other seas,
Annihilating all that's made
To a green thought in a green shade.

Annihilating all that's made. That's what it was, annihilation, and Mrs. Liddell for some reason seemed to pick that part of it up. She did not find him charming.

⚘

Photography required greater physical discipline than any of Dodgson's previous undertakings, and he was aware of all of the things that could go wrong in the process: any movement during the forty-five seconds or so it took to take a photograph—a breeze, a change in temperature, a fluctuation of light, a shadow, a fleck of lint—could fatally mar the print. He still had to remind himself of the steps. First he had to pour the gummy collodion, a mixture of guncotton and ether, over the 8x10 or 3x4 glass plate, which he had already rubbed and polished, careful to coat it evenly. Then he had to dip it in the silver nitrate solution. That done, he had to rush the plate back to the camera. If it dried before he got there, if the sleeve of his jacket scraped against it, if his concentration slipped for a second, he would have to start over. After exposing the plate by opening the camera and then closing it for the correct amount of time, he had to hurry to the darkroom, where he would balance the plate in his hands, pour developing solution over it, straining it off into a bottle, and then apply the fixing solution. Afterward, he had to heat the plate evenly before varnishing, draining, and drying it. A laborious process, one might say, to gather images of scenery you see every day. But still, it was astonishing when the view emerged out of egg whites and silver nitrates. To create a universe out of sticky whiteness. In the beginning he was in love with anything that collided with the viewfinder: the distance he wanted from the world conjured in the lens.

❧

George Macdonald had longish black hair that radiated in all directions—he liked to run his fingers through it—a wild black beard brightened by strands of russet and gray, and small oak-brown eyes, all of which contributed to the paradox of his appearance, which was both bearlike and shy. He had dropped by Dodgson's rooms and squeezed his large frame into the mahogany armchair by the window.

Macdonald was balancing a whiskey and soda on his knee.

"So I hear you've taken quite a fancy to the Liddell's governess."

"Miss Prickett?"

"So I hear."

Dodgson was silent.

"From whom?"

"No shame in it. She is a pretty girl from what I've heard."

Macdonald swirled his drink, gold shards of flame reflected in the glass.

Dodgson felt the heat prickling his face. He felt as guilty as if it had been true, though nothing was further from the truth. He found Miss Prickett—round, downy-armed, wide-hipped—more than faintly off-putting. But in truth, he hadn't given her much thought. She was almost a noise in his head, a buzzing sound, calling the children to bed, telling them to fix the collars on their dresses, in the background of his visits to the Liddells.

How had the rumor started? Simply the sheer amount of time he spent with the children? The idea of their being talked about, his name and hers entwined, floating through the university, into the rooms of students he barely knew, appalled him. He had never before done anything to get himself talked about and it bewildered him, the intimacy of gossip. He felt helpless, his intentions twisted, made sordid and ridiculous.

"I assure you. There is absolutely no truth to it."

"As you wish." Macdonald grinned.

The topic, Dodgson realized, was closed. Even his friend George could not be brought around to the truth. Any protestation only confirmed the delicacy of a secret flirtation. There was a logical loop he was stuck in: people in love affairs deny their love affairs. He had to deny this love affair. He had a quick vision of himself and Miss Prickett pressed against each other in the dark gleaming curves of the kitchen and wondered how anyone in their right mind could believe it. But it was not just a question of him. Her reputation was at stake. Had she heard the rumors? Had Mrs. Liddell?

A sip of sherry ran warm and spicy down his throat.

"No need to take it quite so much to heart," Macdonald said. "Everyone is always out for a bit of scandal."

The wind rattled the window.

Macdonald opened a cracked leather folder and took out a page covered in painful scratches and revisions in blue ink: his latest poems for Dodgson to read.

Dodgson tried to concentrate on the clever poem about a turtle, which was a metaphor for loneliness.

November 3, 1856

The camera allows me to consider all angles & possibilities—to contemplate beauty—as in perfection of form—the size of an ankle—the width of a waist—the narrowness of hips. Grown women drift farther & farther from that ideal form—fatter & broader—the lines are ruined, the angles obscured, the curves made too pronounced. Perhaps no man looks at a grown woman without searching for traces of her fallen beauty—her former perfection—the smooth shadow of what she once was passing across her blighted form.

Though I cannot deny that many of my friends seem to view the ladies of their acquaintance as aesthetic creatures: Reginald Southey has taken to hovering around the deanery & cultivating friendships with the girls for the sole purpose of ingratiating himself with Mrs. Liddell. And then of course there is Rossetti—

what about the sad ethereal figure in Ecce Ancilla
Domini? She is beautiful with her burnt gold hair and
wide eyes—her gaunt, angular face—her narrow
form—as if she has been surviving on wind—but she is
beautiful insofar as she is not of this world. His creations bear no resemblance to the sturdy, earthbound
women I see strolling through Ch. Ch.

It is a truly difficult aesthetic problem—how to take
the flesh out of a woman—the fat, the curve—& leave
the beauty of soul—the perfect reflection of God's intentions. If we take seriously that women were created
out of Adam's rib, then what is closer to that sleek perfection of rib, the woman or the child?

3

Mrs. Liddell had sent the maid over to Dodgson's rooms with pink lilies from the garden. They were left over from Alice's seventh birthday party the day before, which he had attended along with half of the college. Dodgson had never understood the phrase happy birthday. As far as he was concerned, birthdays and happiness were mutually exclusive. He had watched Alice lean over the cake, hair sliding in front of her face. Even the rituals surrounding birthdays were alarming and unfestive, he thought, like the extinguishing of flame. Afterward he had taken her aside and told her he would give her an "un-birthday" present on a different day so as not to encourage her to get any older.

Mrs. Liddell could not know his extreme aversion to cut flowers, but still; their perfume hung in the air, thick and sugary, marking their own funerals. Flowers seemed almost the worst present anyone could give to anyone else. But then he knew most people didn't feel that way. He put them in a blue and white Chinese vase by the window. But he knew what was going to happen. He wouldn't be able to throw them away, would helplessly watch the brown creep through the pink, in spidery lines, until the flowers were utterly claimed.

Dodgson ducked through the faded velvet curtain to get to the darkroom, the chemical-scented darkness surrounding and soothing him. He began printing the photographs he had taken of Alice's birthday, spilling the thick mixture of egg whites and nitrates over the paper and pressing it against the plate.

He thought of Alice turning seven. He added and multiplied her by herself. He thought of her turning fourteen, and then forty-nine, then three hundred and forty-three, a column of figures flying down the page. He thought of the Manchester Giant who had been in the papers. His mother complained to the newspaper about having to mend the buttons and tears in his shirts every week.

He had not meant to take the photograph of Alice crying. But there it was, Alice crushed. The afternoon had been flawless, blue sky, pineapple ices, tables set up in the garden, children squalling out of pure jealousy. He had been feeling isolated in front of a plate of untouched, flamboyantly pink cake. He couldn't help but calculate his importance to the Liddells by the number of people seated closer to them than him (31). And so he had slipped off to the side to take photographs, to dip his head into the calico curtain and surround himself in darkness. But somewhere in the crowd—women in muslin, children smeared with pink icing—the French china doll lay neglected in her tissue. And her face, with real eyelashes and lids that came down over painted blue eyes, was smashed into pieces by a careless boot. He heard the crunch and saw the pale thing, lying with its shattered and caved-in face, its perfect nose hanging to the left.

Dodgson took Alice's tears more personally than he had ever taken anyone's tears, or anyone's feelings of any kind. The whole experience was abrupt and dislocating. He did not feel sorry for her. He felt the doll smashing in his chest as if it had happened to him. The frantic excitement of the party, the quick chemical conversion of mood. He had heard of people feeling this way before, of course. But he must have been peculiarly selfish to have reached the age of twenty-seven and never once experienced someone else's emotion as his own.

That was why he took the photograph. To keep something of himself that he had never seen before. He wrote the number carefully down on the back, neg. 206 1/3 and pasted it into his album.

August 15, 1859

Four o'clock. Bronze light.

Finally managed to borrow Alice for a series of portraits—without the others. She was quite excited at the prospect & we began straightaway without the usual game-playing.

I splattered my trousers with collodion & nitrates running back & forth from the darkroom, black spackled & strange smelling. Alice laughed.

I seemed to be always in motion, as did Alice. I found myself running back & forth to the darkroom to coat the glass plate in collodion, dip it in silver nitrate,

*carrying it carefully back—with Alice darting behind
the screen to change costume—From the beginning
there was a rhythm—I covered the lens—she was a
beggar girl—covered the lens—she was a Chinaman—
covered again—she was a gypsy—& all the while I was
running back & forth to the darkroom so as not to lose
the precious images. But as we were running & she was
changing—as if she was losing her physical form
through the sheer speed of transformation—beggar girl,
Chinaman, gypsy—Develop, fix, varnish—She rose
above her circumstances—Oxford, 1859, my rooms
above the old library—& became part of the ether—& I
rose out of mine. We were playing a higher game, above
the confines of who we were—no longer the pale stutterer, the stooped & desiccated Mr. Dodgson & a little
girl with hair falling into her eyes—but two beings
changing & fluttering above the earth.*

*She stood behind the rice-paper screen & I watched
her shadow squatting & wriggling with the costumes—
throwing a black lace-up shoe onto the rug—carelessly
shaken off of her foot—the shadow made flesh—I
wanted to see her, not through the accidental sag &
drape of clothing, but truly see her—A little piece of
walking art—Nymph in the garden—Fairy in the
woods—Innocent frolicking—Smelling of grass & river
wind & cat hairs—A stretch of milky stomach—Dark,
dirty Alice, never managing to be straightened and neat
like Ina or sweet like Edith—Olive skinned,
Mediterranean—a changeling—Something that has
flown or fallen from somewhere else.*

*Consider the beggar girl—Look at the rags falling off
her delicate shoulders—hand on hips, head cocked—look
at how bewitching she is—her legs slender—her feet too
long like a puppy's—stripped down to her essence—torn
clothes, dirt—somehow more Alice than all of the lace
and ribbons—the wide-sleeved muslins and velvets in
which her mother wraps her up like an offering to fash-
ion—Her eyebrows raised slightly—she is ragged,
bedraggled—her skin luminous but splotched with dirt—
as if she has seen the world—has seen more than an innocent who has barely left Oxford possibly could have.*

*I am astonished by the imminence of transforma-
tion—one can see it quivering in the photograph—her
impatience, her restlessness—as if she has found her
life tiresome—Miss Prickett & geography & piano lessons & tea—one can see the heat of her unhappiness
rising off the photograph—her desire so palpable—to
be & not just appear to be some creature other than
what she is.*

The wooden banister across the upstairs gallery of the
deanery was carved with lions, which were part of the Liddell
family crest. Behind it was Alice, crouching on the landing in
her nightgown. She was supposed to be saying her prayers, but
Miss Prickett was downstairs gossiping with the cook and Alice
had run out when she heard the door.

"Thank you so much for coming, Mr. Dodgson."

"It's my p-p-pleasure." She heard the familiar voice drift
upward. Nervous.

Though she had known him as long as she could remember, an unlikely glamour had begun to settle on the mathematical lecturer. Her father was not interested in her. He was interested in her. His focus felt warm like a lamp suddenly lit in a dark room, a pool of creamy unexpected light. She liked his stories where things came zigzagging out of nowhere, each minute unconnected to the next. True, she was not sure if he was quite like other people. If he were her own age, stuttering like that, she would certainly not like him. And then there was her mother's voice when she talked to him, which always seemed too sweet and layered, like the French desserts the cook served, as if she felt bad for not liking him more. Her mother had once told Lorina to be especially nice to Mr. Dodgson at a breakfast party because he had difficulty in social settings. Will he ever get married? Edith asked. I don't think so, darling, her mother said. If there were something wrong with him, even something to be disapproved of, Alice did not hold it against him. He made her feel like the line between adults and children was as imaginary as the equator. Invented and believed in out of convenience, but not physical fact. The other day he went on his knees with her in the dirt in the cook's garden, acting out a scene between the tomato vines and the peas, croaking out strange lines in the character of the tomato: *My vegetable love should grow vaster than empires, and more slow.*

She called him nothing. She had no name for him. If she was forced to address him she would call him Mr. Dodgson, of course, but she never did. It seemed overly formal for the man on his knees with her in the dirt of the cook's garden, a narrow leaf caught in his hair. And there was the glamour: the prickly, charged vagueness that surrounded the question of who he was.

Alice squeezed her face through the bars of the stairway so she could see the top of her mother's lacquered brown head bent over the photographs. If she looked carefully she could make out the tiny white blotch on the photograph that must be her.

When Dodgson came to take those photographs, he had asked for her sisters too, but it was understood between them that it was her he wanted. Their friendship was structured like a private joke: everybody could hear it, but only they understood what it meant.

Alice liked the darkroom best; she liked standing close to him in the tiny, crowded room, surrounded by brown bottles of strange-smelling liquid, concentrating on not knocking anything over, watching him pour the chemicals and heat the glass, her face appearing out of nowhere, but reversed: her skin charred black, her eyes white, her dress black, her hair white.

Afterward she had stood on his sofa in her stockinged feet and looked at his gold-framed map of the world. Alice loved maps. She loved the bright pinks and blues. She loved the names of oceans, Caspian, Dead Sea, Atlantic, the triangles that were mountains, the blue threads that were rivers, the heart that was Africa, the pointed boot that was Italy.

Mrs. Liddell was not enthusiastic about the beggar-girl photograph. In the dark parlor, with its heavy wine-colored drapes and damask wallpaper, the black and whiteness of the photographs was somehow more pronounced. The contrasts leapt out. The torn white dress, gaping at the chest and falling off the shoulders of its small model, seemed more conspicuous.

Dodgson slipped the beggar girl to the bottom of the pile and quickly moved to a pretty profile—ruffled dress with wide sleeves, a wreath of flowers around her head.

"May I see the other one again?" asked Mrs. Liddell.

Dodgson had no choice. He handed the beggar-girl photograph to her and leaned back against a stiff needlework cushion.

Mrs. Liddell studied the photo. Against rough stone leaned her dirty-faced daughter, draped in rags, torn, unraveling. She had one hand on her hip, the other compliantly cupped. Such a convincing urchin. But there was something else. The picture glowed with a joke that had just been told. She could see it in her daughter's eyes, laughter dying down.

"Quite pretty," she said, smiling. But she was uneasy. In a book she had just finished, *The Banker's Wife,* the daughter Ellen becomes an actress, a protégée of the barracks, and this is what happens to her mother: *The poor woman, long harassed by anxiety, poverty, and care, laid her head on the pillow of sickness and never lifted it again. Her next resting place was the grave.* Mrs. Liddell knew that it was ridiculous to work herself into a state about a photograph. But there was something wrong, something almost womanly and seductive in Alice's leaning back like that, and she couldn't tell if it was coming from Alice or from the unseen camera. If it was trick of costume and light. But there seemed to be an exchange, an electric flow, that the photograph was only partly picking up. She wanted the outer frame of the photograph to expand to include Mr. Dodgson hunched behind his camera. She knew she could derive what was happening from the three inches of forehead. She wanted to see *him.*

Was it possible for the future to furtively enter a photograph and illuminate it? She felt like the camera had gotten at the essence of Alice, mischievous, sultry, but it was the essence of a future grown-up Alice.

It suddenly occurred to her that Dodgson had never once asked to take her picture. Even as they sat there on the sofa together, inches apart, there was a complete absence of the usual tension. He had come to show her the photographs out of a sense of obligation, she realized; they were not like the meditations on Aristotle or toy boats for the children or other offerings she was used to receiving from her husband's protégés. Most of the young men who came to the house were attentive to the children to get at her. Was it possible that Dodgson was polite to her to get at the children?

Dodgson put his cup on the table.

Mrs. Liddell turned back to the photograph of the beggar girl. The image compelled her, she had to admit. The photograph showed the way in which Alice was beautiful. Sometimes you couldn't see her particular beauty in normal light—she looked sallow, scrawny, dark—but you could see it here.

Sometimes, in Alice's growing loveliness she saw a mirror of her own decline: the lines across her forehead, the dry, crepey skin on her face, the few gray hairs, the small circle of fat around her stomach that hadn't bothered her at first because it had come with the children. But these were not appropriate thoughts for a mother, she quickly told herself, and tried to push them out of her mind. What was left was a trace of irritation.

"Cake?" She pushed the orange sponge cake in Dodgson's direction.

"No, thank you." He looked faintly alarmed.

She put the photographs down on the table next to a chubby porcelain goddess.

"Well, Mr. Dodgson," she said finally. "I don't know what to say. I am quite overwhelmed. I am sure very few children are so lucky as to have every mood and angle documented by such a talented photographer."

"P-p-please." Dodgson shifted uneasily. "Take whichever ones you would like."

He watched as Mrs. Liddell selected several of the more formal portraits. Then, after a moment's hesitation, she took the beggar girl too.

Mrs. Liddell leaned against the doorway and watched him walk down the path. She would be the first to admit that her fears were irrational—it was perfectly acceptable, in fact, extremely fashionable to have a photographer do dress-up portraits of little girls, but she was worried. True, he was a man who went into London to see art shows, had friends in artistic circles, and cared more about light and form and composition than any other side of life. His pale features were so carefully devoid of emotion, so correctly empty of anything but thought. His eyes were gray and smooth like the inside of a church.

But there was something odd in his manner. She felt it the way a mother can feel any threat to her children, when it is only a remote possibility, a book that might fall, a table's sharp edge that might cut; she felt the invisible potential of the situation, the magnificence of the beggar-girl photograph, as a kind of heaviness in her chest.

4

Dr. James Hunt was tall and stooped, but his narrow face, with its prominent nose, thick eyebrows and small pebble-colored eyes, was nondescript. What was extraordinary about him was his voice, which rumbled through a room, low and rich.

"Hello, Dodgson," the voice came from behind the desk. It seemed a mockery that a speech specialist should have such a voice.

Hunt's study was small. There was a shiny mahogany sofa with curled arms and lion-claw feet next to a cast-iron standing lamp. On the wall next to the door was a scientific diagram of a man's head and throat, with emanating lines that looked like pins in a voodoo doll, labeling: *pharynx, uvula, cranium.* On his desk was a large bird skeleton under glass, and the mantel above the fireplace was lined with jars filled with sea creatures. The faint smell of salt and brine made Dodgson seasick.

"I hope I fare better than the bird," said Dodgson, sitting on the sofa.

"No one does."

A liver-and-white spaniel was sprawled out under the desk.

Hunt launched into his elaborate theory of The Stutter, with which Dodgson was only vaguely familiar. Hunt was rumored to be working on the definitive book on the subject, called *Stammering and Stuttering*. With each stutterer, Hunt explained, the culprit was either the tongue, the breathing, the lips or the jaw. And in each case, there was a treatment: reading fast or slow, breathing differently, or holding the tongue in a specific position in the mouth. This practical approach had been pioneered by his father, Thomas Hunt, in a blaze of controversy and success, and refined and elucidated and intellectualized by himself after a few years of medical study.

Hunt stretched out his legs and crossed his ankles.

Leaves flattened against the window in the wind.

"Nobody stutters by chance," Hunt said. "They stutter by design."

In Dodgson's case, he believed the problem might be the jaw. He also believed that Dodgson was holding a large part of himself back. That he was trying to keep a secret with the stutter. That there was something he didn't want to say. An unwillingness, a willful desire, that added an additional stumbling block to fluid speech.

Sometimes, Dodgson thought, people like Hunt sprout up here, in the environs of Oxford, for lack of sun, lack of oxygen, lack of exposure to real life. They have too much time to think, so a mere quirk of biology or fate becomes a fraught intellectual problem; the quirk takes on all sorts of shadings and meanings, because if it didn't he would be bored to death sitting under his heavy leather books and voice diagrams and bird skeletons. Still . . . holding back. Not saying. As if there were a struggle on a day-to-day, sentence-by-sentence, word-by-word level: not to reveal.

"In some cases, stuttering can be a natural extension of the shy temperament," Hunt explained.

"I am not sure if that is correct, in my case," Dodgson protested. "I am quite the opposite of shy these days."

In Dodgson's own mind he socialized constantly and shallowly. He felt, at least, like he was always pushing himself forward. Standing up in front of students, for one thing. Babbling on to colleagues at breakfast. It is true he had a flash of terror whenever he entered a roomful of people, but over the years he had managed to create a mannered, relatively gregarious persona to compensate for it.

"Tell me about Daresbury," Hunt said.

"What is there to tell?" Dodgson said. "It was a small parish in the country. Twice a day prayers. Cold food on Sundays. Clerical politics and prying old ladies. Nothing you haven't read in Trollope."

But that wasn't it at all. Daresbury was ivy splashed across the modest two-story brick house and the smell of jasmine. Daresbury was the faded chintz sofa by the lace-curtained window that his mother lay in constantly, with yet another baby in her arms. Daresbury was his father's voice echoing angrily through the house, complaining about the money spent on the trellis in the garden. And the flowered vase from his aunt Lucy

45

Lutwidge that was swept off the sideboard in that anger. His father had not thrown it, had not hurled it at his mother; he had knocked it over accidentally, his limbs large and sweeping; but in that clumsy fury, something had to break. The five-year-old could see the shatter in his mother's face. The little pieces of porcelain glistening on the floor. The flowers and leaves curling off into oblivion. Daresbury was his father's rules. No hot food on Sundays. No puppet theaters on Sundays. No theatergoing ever. There were rules about when to eat and what, prayers in the morning, in the cold, when you are still mostly asleep, your feet like ice on the floor, saying the words, each one containing him, your father. And there deep beneath them, the wander. That was Dodgson's response. Sitting on the floor scribbling notes for a play in the margin of his Latin books, a tragedy in three parts. His thoughts doodled, and created; they formed themselves into cartoons and rhymes.

Dodgson couldn't figure out what the small house he grew up in had to do with the stutter. Perhaps Hunt was trying to get him to blather on so that he could see when he started stuttering. Perhaps he was trying to isolate the exact moment eloquence slipped away from him.

"I like to know my patients," Hunt said. "Try to regard our conversations as twenty years of leisurely acquaintance condensed into a few months."

"Sounds quite exhausting."

"Yes, well, that's the point."

"Because if one is tired one stutters more?"

"I find people stutter more over the most familiar material. Over the stories that are oldest," Hunt said. "I also find it helpful to know when the stuttering began."

"Like Wordsworth's line, *The child is father of the man?*"

"Exactly."

And so, like the dutiful student he had been and still was, Dodgson began to tell Hunt about his father, the Reverend Charles Dodgson, brilliant, leonine, and broad-chested, in his black clergyman's robes, his polished shoes. Dodgson remembered one day when he had been allowed to accompany him to the druggist. The reverend's eminence trailed behind them through the town like the tail of a comet, people taking off their hats as they passed. When they got to the store, the reverend left his son standing underneath crowded shelves of tonics and ointments, while he went to talk to the druggist. Dodgson saw one of the clerks eye his father and say to another: *He can't seem to keep his hands off her, can he?* There were so many children in so few years. Dodgson felt a deep shame flow through him. There were too many of them, visible signs of sin, fleshly manifestations of unspeakable acts. *He can't seem to keep his hands off her.* A few weeks later a baby died. This was hard to piece together as a child, to stitch together some kind of sense out of these equally unmanageable facts, his parents not being able to keep their hands off each other, his newborn sister's death.

And then there was his father's unspoken, unbreathed about disappointment. The sense of loss drifted through the entire house and dragged everyone in, the compromise his father had made with his own brilliance. The loss was there at the dinner table, a tension that held and fascinated them, entering into the smallest exchanges, one person passing the gravy to another, a drop spilling on the tablecloth, and his father raging coolly against the offender. Nothing can be undone. Not a brown spot on white cloth. Not a man frittering away his intelligence in a remote parish for very little money. Not a large family that kept getting larger. He remembered his mother disappearing for her laying in. Her stomach, half glimpsed through slipping blanket, hard and egglike and swollen. She would be swept away, wrapped in the whispers of servants. He remembered creeping down the hallway toward her bedroom, where he had been directly forbidden to go, and hearing pans crashing and servants speaking rapidly in low tones. Sometime later, he would be allowed to see his baby sister in the nursery, swaddled, pink-faced, turkey-necked, with a horrible black down on its dented head. Twice there had been no baby. This interested and appalled him: the disappearance of the large cloth-swaddled flesh of his mother's stomach into nothingness. The fact that flesh could be converted into air. The quiet afterward.

He knew that his father had given up the coveted studentship at Christ Church, Oxford, to marry his mother. You couldn't have that prestigious position and be married, and his father, who cared so much about prestige and positions, chose marriage. There was something sinful in it, Dodgson would come to feel later, something carnal and distasteful in his deciding to step down and surrender his highest principles and lifelong aspirations for a wife, for a warm nightgowned woman in his bed, emerging from sleep, her hair brushed out, loose and messy and curling, a red-gold netting around her face, her fleshy arms emerging from her nightgown. His father left Oxford for those arms, for the embrace of those arms, for procreation, for the irresistible multiplication of self. Frances Jane, Elizabeth Lucy, Charles Lutwidge, Caroline Hume, Mary

Charlotte, Skeffington Hume, Wilfred Longley, Louisa Fletcher, Margaret Anne Ashley, Henrietta Harington, Edwin Heron. Eleven children and two ghosts.

Some small portion of this was related without stuttering once to Hunt, who, when it was over, suggested that he read a section of *A Midsummer Night's Dream*, act two, scene i, over to himself three times quickly each day.

5

Alice was sitting on Dodgson's lap on the old rocking chair in the nursery with her arm draped around his neck. The room was relatively bare, with only an oak table covered with a crocheted doily, a round rag rug, and a standing chalkboard by the door. The winter sun shone through the lace curtain, casting a latticed pattern, half-moons of light, on the floor. He was telling her a story. He was speaking softly, without stuttering. *But wait a bit, the oyster cried, before we have our chat. For some of us are out of breath and all of us are fat.* His voice was thick, fibrous. She was lost in it, as if every part of her were broken up and carried away. She was the oyster, the sun, the walrus. Her hand was on his neck and she could feel the words, the stretch of tendon as he spoke. Like an instrument almost. The oysters, the walrus, the carpenter, the crazy march by the sea forming itself in rhyme just for her. She melted against his chest, oysterlike herself.

Alice felt his legs underneath her, more fragile and birdlike than her father's. She played with his collar as he spoke. She knew he was telling the story just for her, that he was making each moment up to please her. Oysters wearing shoes. Her mother served oysters at a party. He anticipated her desires even before she knew what they were, and she felt her presence in the story itself, her imprint on its invisible, muscular form. *I weep for you, the walrus said: I deeply sympathize. With sobs and tears he sorted out those of the largest size.* What does Alice want? She could feel Dodgson thinking as he spoke, underneath, and that question, that anticipation was it: her participation. The ideas thrown up from the depths just for her. This was something she understood right from the beginning, the collaboration of the story. These stories were not just for her, they were *from* her.

In the end all of the good-natured oysters were eaten by the walrus and carpenter, their shells staring up blankly from the hot sand. A desolate ending, some might have thought. But Alice couldn't stop laughing.

❦

Dodgson walked quickly down the street with his umbrella. He turned right and headed toward Trafalgar Square, the dark gray splotches in the sky threatening rain. He had a slightly pleasurable headache from one too many glasses of red wine at a dinner party at the Macdonalds' the night before, and the street sounds were muffled and cottony. Just the perfect mood for the Royal Academy, he thought to himself. He had come to London for a few days to see the collective exhibit of new photographs but had put it off until his last few hours.

The crowds fanned out at the entrance, trying to get in. The year before there had been almost no one. Lady Eastlake's recent essay had breathlessly declared photography "a new form of communication" and "a household word." This peculiar hobby of his had caught on, and he didn't know how he felt about it. He had no interest in communicating.

Dodgson drifted slowly through the great hall, looking at hands. In his own photographs, hands gave him trouble. All of his sitters' self-consciousness somehow flowed into their hands, he was not sure why. He stopped for a minute at the space where his "Little Red Riding Hood" had hung. A willow in front of a brick house hung there now, technically adequate but unexciting. Four of his photographs had appeared in the Royal Academy's exhibition the year before: "Little Red Riding Hood," "Portrait," "Group of Children from Life," and "Portrait of a Child." And since then many of his prints had circulated through more casual channels, passed around by the parents of children whose portraits he had taken: the Welds, the Macdonalds, the Marshalls, the Tidys, the Hobsons, the Henleys, and the Tennysons, among others. A modest myth was rising up around him in certain circles—the strange Oxford don who takes portraits of children and poets. But he felt strangely detached from his new prominence, as if it were a *carte de visite* from another country, shown to you by a friend who has been vacationing there.

In fact, the Photographic Society had approached him about hanging his new photographs in this exhibit, but he had politely declined. He had decided that portraits looked gaudier under glass, the sheen catching the light, forcing the subject to compete with the reflection. And the idea of Alice on the wall was impossible.

Ladies in large hats bent around the framed photographs. His mood was slipping. He knew that his new photographs were good, better than most of those hanging. But somehow that knowledge gave him no pleasure. As he roamed restlessly through the gallery he was surprised at how much he craved the space, how busy his mind was replacing the exhibition photographs with his own. He couldn't help feeling like what he was seeing hung on the walls, in heavy gilt frames and sad sepia, was his own desire to impress. He was not a photographer, he reminded himself, he was a mathematician with a hobby.

With these thoughts running through his mind, he didn't see Gertrude Thomson until she was right in front of him, shapeless and slouching, her mousy hair disheveled under a gray silk bonnet. She carried an umbrella, a sketch pad, and pens. She was a moderately successful children's book illustrator. He had been impressed by her black and white fairies and nymphs.

"Have you seen these?" She gestured toward the photographs by a famous lady photographer, whose profiles of young women with faraway eyes and cascading hair had become all the rage.

"Yes," Dodgson said quietly, but he had been avoiding them.

"Marvelous, aren't they?" She brushed the strands of hair out of her face and looked straight at him. "Or are her models too old for you?"

"I should say so." Dodgson smiled. "Decrepit."

She had seen his new photographs, then. Someone whose children he had photographed must have shown them to her. Perhaps the Tennysons.

"I feel the same way," she said. "I generally sketch girls under ten."

"I find seven the most sublime."

"I catch them wherever I can. The seaside is one of my most successful hunting grounds. I find it's easier to capture anatomical grace in bathing costumes."

A vision came to him of waves lapping the sunbrowned legs of three small girls.

"Lovely to run into you," she said suddenly, then wiggled her fingers at him, turned, and vanished into the crowd.

On the train ride home he scribbled this on a piece of paper he then folded into his jacket pocket:

> I must say that the great lady's photographs do
> not impress me. They are excessively romantic—
> somehow cannot focus on the loveliness of their
> subjects. All doom & misery & large heads. They are
> not natural & that is what I don't care for. The great-
> est advantage one has in photographing children is
> nature. One need not make them all so haunted.
> Every single one of her unfortunate subjects looks
> as if they had just witnessed the dismembering of a
> favorite pet. The light is indirect & moody—always
> the peculiar light of a storm—& the portraits are not
> portraits of the girls so much as the artist's state of
> mind. I hate this kind of self-promotion in photogra-
> phers. There is something to aspire to: Remember to

include the person you are photographing in the photograph.

⚜

Mrs. Liddell's mind was damp and tropical from reading. Pounding hearts. Secret rendezvous in the park. She put her copy of *The Widow and the Marquess* by Mr. Theodore Hook down on the bed table. On the page she had just finished, the widowed Mrs. Franklin believes that the affluent Mr. Smith is about to ask her to marry him, only Mr. Smith actually wants to marry her daughter Harriet, who is thirty years younger than he is and in love with the penniless Mr. Carville. The candle next to the brass bed sliced the room into dark gold stripes. The chintz curtains were drawn; huge dark roses tumbled down the wallpaper. The world was suddenly heightened and tragic and important-seeming, as if everything were star-dotted and misty and brilliant, every word uttered passionately and ardently, every china silk off-the-shoulder dress, with rose trim and flounces, falling in flattering folds. She was in one of those moods. Largely manufactured by Mr. Theodore Hook and the publishers of the Railway Novels.

She turned to her husband.

"Henry."

She wanted to talk.

"Henry?"

He was asleep. He hadn't even bothered to get under the covers. She suddenly felt the intimacy of sitting next to him on the bed. His naked chest, arms, the heft of his thighs. She loved how substantial he was. The sprawl of him. The embrace that might have been was tangible in the air: her desire and his lack of desire, incontrovertible facts that stood like the eight-foot rosewood armoire and the marble washstand on the other side of the room. Henry had not been paying much attention to her lately, he was so caught up in his reforms. The workmen's cottages he was planning to put up along the edges of Christ Church, for instance. He couldn't stop talking about them, the plans, the construction, the million minor controversies that she could recite by memory. He hadn't touched her in weeks. Even during the day, he was distracted. The Leonardo da Vinci of our university, people called him. In fact, Mrs. Lamb had told her just that morning that she had seen him halfway down a drainpipe. She was not surprised, as there was no aspect of university maintenance or tinkering so small that the dean would not involve himself. So much the public man he was unable to be a man in private. A catalog of minor annoyances ran through her head: He had forgotten to comment on her new satin-trimmed bonnet from London, hadn't given the skittish cook enough praise after dinner.

Her husband's breathing was deep and innocent, and for a moment she felt guilty. Here he was, forehead vulnerable through thinning hair, eyelids almost transparent, delicate and babyish, with thin blue veins running through them, long reddish eyelashes. She could smell him, the rich, musky bookish smell of him, or what she associated when she was younger with books but later came to understand was just his natural, unbathed smell. He disturbed her, stretching out like a graceful animal. His grace disturbed her.

There were conversations she was somehow waiting to have, an exchange of information where they really took each other into their days. She wanted to tell him, for instance, about her ladies' reading group discussion of Homer's Penelope and ask him whether he thought it was quite normal that the mathematical lecturer should spend so much time with the children. Yes, that was one of the things she wanted to talk to him about: what he really thought about Charles Dodgson, what complicated gradations of thought lay behind his politic heartiness. Her husband acted the same way toward every young man who passed through the university, a friendly, warm bluster with a center of coolness so subtle she was the only one who could sense it, so it was hard to know which ones he really liked. It never occurred to him to talk about people on his own, but when she pressed him, she discovered he had assessed and analyzed and footnoted the person in question as thoroughly as one of his Greek words.

She put her arm lightly around his stomach. She felt the warmth pooled in the sheet next to him and huddled into it. He shifted toward her but continued to sleep. He was probably dreaming about drainpipes.

6

Alice was riding a pony with her father. Dodgson arrived at the meadow just in time to see them trotting off. She was bouncing along on the chestnut pony, holding herself stiffly. Still small for a ten-year-old. Dodgson knew this was one of her favorite things to do, to ride next to her father's gray stallion. Even though she was facing the other way he could tell she was flushed with pleasure. He knew that this was one of the few times she saw her father, one of the few things he would deign to do with her. Of course he was her father, and it was perfectly natural for her to feel attached to him, but suddenly Dodgson felt unappreciated. Her father darted ahead and she followed, the pony almost slipping out from under her she kicked him so hard. How much harder it is to tell stories, how much more is required, thought Dodgson, than simply bouncing up and down on a horse saying nothing but "good girl" and "take another go!"

Dodgson realized he might be the only man in Oxford who didn't like the dean. Liddell was the paragon of the English gentleman, or so everyone said, but what that really meant was that he was thinking about something else when he spoke to you. He expanded deliberately into a type; his was a politician's skill, smoothing away the edges and particularities of self. He reminded Dodgson of the boys at school who stayed up all night studying for exams but then pretended they had done no work at all. He had that same studied nonchalance. Dodgson didn't like the heartiness in his voice, which made it seem as if every conversation about philosophy and lexicography were going to deteriorate into a discussion of which wine goes best with lamb. The dean actually called the main stairway in the deanery "the lexicon," after his immensely lucrative but unimaginative treatise on Greek, which paid for his personal renovations. How vulgar, Dodgson thought. How inadvertently suggestive of lovely little girls trampling the pages of that great work every time they went to bed.

He couldn't help thinking of all the ways the dean was trying to destroy the university, and he didn't think that was too strong a way of putting it. There were the stained-glass windows he had already taken out, the modern bay windows he had put in, the entryway to the cathedral he had changed and lowered. He thought of what would happen if he took all of the old pinnacles and spires of Oxford and tried to rub them smooth of history and character. A travesty, taking everything grand and mysterious about the university and chipping away at it until all that remained was grim, modern anonymity.

Even worse was the clock tower the dean was planning, with the bells encased in a wooden box. In fact, Dodgson thought he might dash off another leaflet of opposition exploring the etymological significance of the new belfry. He would call the style *Early Debased: very early and remarkably debased.* And circulate his leaflet through the campus. He was also considering adding an appendage to his official missive entitled, *Objections Submitted to the Governing Body of Christ Church, Oxford, against Certain Proposed Alterations in the Great Quadrangle.* He realized it sounded harsh, but that is how he felt. It was inconceivable to him that someone would want to create such an aesthetic insult, such an inharmonious tower.

As he stood on the edge of the empty meadow, writing pamphlets about towers in his head, he felt a continuing rage that seemed even to him a bit excessive. Was he perhaps going too far? (The *Oxford Undergraduate Journal* just that month wrote, "The general public enjoys a hearty laugh over the brochures which Mr. Dodgson is continually publishing on these hideous monstrosities.")

He couldn't dispel his mood for hours afterward. He couldn't shake off the picture of Alice and her father galloping off together through the wind-rippled field, with him left behind, tediously on foot.

Dodgson did not usually like reading books aloud, Mrs. Liddell had noticed; he preferred to invent his own nonsense and not to be confined by what he seemed to think were the patently inferior words of a real, professional author. But now, at Alice's urging, he had consented to sit under the willow and read *The Arabian Nights*.

The garden was blowing; Scheherazade was saving her life with stories.

The wind rattled the skinny branches of the willow, and Mrs. Liddell tightened the shawl around her shoulders.

Her daughters were draped over Dodgson to get a better view of the illustrations. She was scrutinizing Dodgson himself. A pale almost chalky complexioned man with a long face, carefully parted hair with a curl at the ends. His usually sad gray eyes were lit up by the story, and the anxious lines around his mouth were gone. He was holding the book in one hand and sculpting the features of the veiled lady in the air with the other. The girls were entranced. Her husband seemed to think Dodgson was infatuated with Miss Prickett. But that was clearly not the case. She wondered why Miss Prickett's charms came so quickly into her husband's head. She looked again at Dodgson's hair. For a man who took such great care to dress correctly, to conform to the fashions of the times, at least Oxford's interpretations thereof, his hair was just a little too long, a little curling, feminine. He wasn't simply careless, Mrs. Liddell was sure of that. He was making a deliberate choice. His hair was an aesthetic statement of some kind, as everything he did seemed to be. She looked at them forged together like a living statue, four bent heads, dark shoulder-length hair.

Mrs. Liddell was not fond of womanish men. In her mind, that was what was wrong with Oxford—with the exception of her husband, of course—the men were not men. They were fragile somehow, damaged. The boys were better, but not much and not always.

Later that evening, Mrs. Liddell stood in the doorway of the nursery.

"Miss Prickett?"

"Yes, ma'am."

"How does Alice seem to you?"

"Well, I think."

"And Mr. Dodgson, has he been around often?"

"Fairly often."

"How do you find him?"

"I am not sure quite what you mean."

"Is there anything at all odd about the way he is acting?"

"Odd?"

Mrs. Liddell said nothing.

"I don't think so. But I cannot be sure."

"The girls are still eager to see him though?"

"Oh, yes. Quite." She flushed.

"What do they do with him for all those hours?"

"Mostly he tells his stories," Miss Prickett said. "They are extraordinary, aren't they?"

"Yes, they are," said Mrs. Liddell, closing the door. She was irritated with herself for trying to get information out of a servant. She was more irritated with herself for failing.

☙

Feb. 4, 1862

This morning I brought a drawing of the walking oysters for Alice, & Mrs. Liddell told me to take it directly to the nursery. On my way back through the hallway, I saw a half-open door. The bath was still drawn—a large oval bath—

I stopped. The floor was damp & the air heavy from steam. Alice must have that moment emerged—running wet and soap-smelling through her room—and there was the bath still filled—the bathwater cloudy with dirt—likely she brought half the garden along with her. The water that had swirled around her legs—splashed her neck—a bar of lavender soap cast carelessly aside—a cloth draped over the side. And I couldn't take my eyes from it—the porcelain curve that had cradled her. Reverberating like an echo: her recently vanished presence.

I felt close to her—wrapped in her—the steam rising up & enveloping me in heat. Her hair sticky damp & plastered to her face—her skin hot—beaded with droplets—her palms pruny & prickled from soaking. The bath gave her to me more vividly than I could have conjured her myself.

So strange. A room caught in a state of longing.

A room abruptly caught—how ridiculous I am—simply an accidentally glimpsed sliver of bath basin through half-open door—& yet it keeps returning.

———

When he came down the stairs, the Liddells were sitting across from each other in the armchairs in front of the fireplace. They were opening letters. Dodgson stood awkwardly in the threshold waiting to take his leave. Was there the subtlest hint of coldness in their manner, or was he imagining it? Perhaps they thought he was taking too many photographs, that his artistic interest was overintense, perhaps his fascination had surpassed even a mother's desire to see the faces of her own children. He did notice the other day that the house was now overflowing with photographs, that there were barely surfaces enough on which to prop any more picture frames. He sensed he was in for a period of isolation. Unwanted guest. The two-headed camera man.

"Please join us, Mr. Dodgson," Mrs. Liddell said finally, looking up from the letters on her lap. But by that time he was so flustered that he mumbled something about having work to do and reached for his hat.

He headed back to his rooms through the courtyard, the silvery stone barely visible through the chaotic snowflakes, which seemed to be flying up from the ground as well as falling from above. He stopped and looked up at the deanery, the crenellated towers looming castlelike against the whitening sky. The nursery window looked blurred through the snow and impossibly far away. An inch of glass, a thousand kilograms of snow, a hundred feet of night, eight inches of wall.

Hours later, he was still bent over his writing table toying with quantities. He felt the same pleasurable ache he had when working on a particularly hard logic problem. How to simplify the situation? Alice was now ten. How to get beyond the limitations of space and time? He began scribbling a new equation, balancing various factors, to solve his relationship with Alice.

$$\frac{A+D}{T\ (a+p+d)} = ?$$

That night he had a dream about Alice. He was sitting on a gold upholstered chair under a cherry blossom tree with Alice on his lap. He could feel her weight on his thighs, her leg swinging against his, the pain of her shoe digging into his shin, her hair brushing against his face, into his mouth, and suddenly her neck started growing. Her head was up in the trees, grown like a horrible serpent, twisting through the branches and into the sky, and she was bigger than him, she was crushing him, and he was getting smaller, and finally she was like a tree herself, her neck a giant barky stalk, and he could no longer see her face.

7

Dr. Hunt was concerned about Dodgson. They had been working together for three years and his stutter was not improving. The tongue-relaxing exercises for his b's and d's were not working. Nor was the daily Shakespeare. If anything his stutter seemed to be getting worse. The words were hostile animals stuck in his throat, his tongue battling his teeth.

And besides the stutter, Dodgson seemed unusually anxious. Any inquiry into his current life, even the most banal questions like "how is your photography coming along?" prompted an almost defensive "quite well thank you." Icy rather. And Dodgson looked paler than usual, if such a thing were possible.

"Whatever it is you are fighting seems to be winning," Hunt said.

"How dramatic," said Dodgson. "It's only a slight fever."

Dodgson was certainly able to dodge.

Dodgson absently fiddled with one of the copies of the *Anthropological Review* on the desk. Hunt had just founded the Anthropological Society and begun editing its monthly journal.

"Darwin enthusiast?" Hunt asked.

"Oh, n-n-no, I don't go in for that kind of thing."

Hunt said, "Let's return to tell the bewilderingly bad boy dinner is delicious."

"Tell the b-b-b-b-," Dodgson began and then stopped. "I'm sorry. I can't manage it today."

"Then tell me what is keeping you up so late at night. I've heard your light is often burning at four in the morning."

"Often, yes."

"Well, surely it isn't Euclid keeping you from sleep."

"No, not Euclid."

"Good," Hunt said, "he's hardly worth it."

"In fact if you must know I've been having d-d-disturbing dreams."

One of Hunt's more advanced treatments was to force his patients to talk about a subject that was hard for them to articulate. He felt such prodding might loosen their speech. If you can talk about the things that are difficult, he often explained to his patients, then you have no trouble with the things that are simple. He had a recent success with one young patient by getting the boy to speak to him in Latin, which happened to be his weakest, most anxiety-provoking subject.

"The d-d-dreams are—well, they are me and not me. I can

hardly explain. They involve a great d-d-deal of growing and shrinking. That sort of thing."

"Are they about anything in particular?"

Dodgson paused.

Hunt suddenly felt like a priest in confession. Though of course Charles Dodgson seemed the least likely candidate for sin in all Oxford. He barely drank, unlike some of the dons; he didn't seem to have a weakness for the fairer sex. Nor did he show any inclinations toward inversion or, as it was now fashionably referred to, the "boy worship" so prevalent in the college. Nonetheless, Hunt felt him trembling on the verge of confession. He felt Dodgson's reserve rise and consolidate like a priest's iron grille between them.

"No, nothing in particular."

Dodgson stood. "Sorry, Hunt. I am afraid I must go. Introductory logic."

"If you ask me," Hunt said, "I think you ought to try Darwin."

Dodgson smiled from the door. "I ought to stop having those bewilderingly bad dreams."

After Dodgson left, Hunt went to the bar, poured himself a whiskey, and settled into his favorite leather chair by the window.

Hunt had begun his practice as a speech specialist to help people function more normally. That was his goal, to help stutterers blend into society. But what he was really interested in were people who didn't blend in. He was interested in the secret flaws and hidden textures of human character. He glanced over at the curling white vertebrae rising from the mess of papers and open books on his desk. What originally attracted him to science was the stripping away and seeing through. But it was harder with people. You have to find your way in through a weakness: a crack, a hole, an opening, yes, a stammer.

Hunt's wife had died seven years earlier delivering a not-quite-right child. The doctor had warned him not to come into the room, but he couldn't help himself. The baby was lying dead on a sheet on the floor, next to a pot of water. Its skin was a beautiful, translucent color, and its—he could not bring himself to say his—eyes were set too wide apart. It was curled up like a sea horse, still protecting its delicate underbelly. The doctor, following Hunt's glance, had quickly scooped the baby up and covered its face, but he couldn't remove the accusation that seemed to hang in the air: the fishchild who had killed his wife had come from somewhere in him.

Since then he had become less interested in the hows of science and more focused on the whys. The shift had affected his practice, his writing, his friendships. He had been honorary secretary of the Ethnographer's Society but had been pushed out because of what some of the members considered his free speculation on man's origins. His work, which had been a pleasant and interesting occupation that he had taken over from his father, began to burn through him.

These days he found himself thinking more and more about Charles Dodgson. Hunt had seen a large number of unusually gifted and oddly unhappy men. Oxford especially hid all sorts of irregularities, attracting men not quite qualified for life outside by some barely perceptible emotional tic. But Dodgson was different, more absorbing.

One of the fascinating things about Dodgson's case was how he functioned as a lecturer. For the most part, since he had started coming to see Hunt, Dodgson managed to get through long, complicated lectures without stuttering. But this may have been achieved through a certain level of detachment, pretending that he was someone else in front of his students. Impersonating an Oxford don. Dodgson once confessed to Hunt that he had a great passion for theater, sneaking off to the princess's theater on Oxford Street, a practice he hid from his father, who objected on religious grounds. He had once told Hunt in an entirely unserious moment that he would have been a fine actor. And that seemed to fit in somehow. As if he went up in front of students in full costume and stage makeup.

Hunt had heard from students that Dodgson's lectures were fantastically boring, but why? Dodgson had shown him a draft of the Euclid dialogues he was working on, and so he knew how brilliantly witty he could be. How wicked. In fact, the most charismatic lecturers in Oxford would have given their right arms for the kind of wit that came naturally to Dodgson, that lay buried in his work, even in his casual, unguarded moments. And yet, he hid it. This level of understatement, or suppression of interest, itself interested Hunt. As if the man were engaged in a deliberate effort to keep the most colorful, appealing parts of himself out of his public presentation. Somehow Dodgson had become the perfectly correct lecturer. The overly strict lecturer. The only lecturer left in all of Oxford who would still make the men copy out lines if they were late.

Hunt watched Dodgson out the window, his brittle stride across the lawn.

May 1862

Saw Hunt & can barely write—this is a mental state with which I am extremely familiar—frustration—the intimate, tiresome knowledge of one's own boundaries—There are times the words do not come into my mouth—the feeling hot behind them—the desire all there—but the words themselves twisted & deformed beyond recognition—tongue tangled against teeth. What if I put them down anyway, mangled as they are, and let the meaning shine through them, in bright pieces, like light through a tree? It matters not what you say—It is the effort, the animating force behind it that signifies—the desire to speak is still there—and that portion of the puzzle will create some modicum of sense. Or so one hopes.

The nightmare is becoming stuck in the stutter, never moving to the next consonant—The words dreaming & dangling—Thought clotted in mind.

This is a feeling I am quite familiar with—Especially in Hunt's study, a dark contentless babble springing up from the depths—It is the sensation of a mathematical paradox beyond my capacities—of story that cannot form into plot. I begin, switch scenes, begin again, switch scenes. There is no sense.

Here lies the distilled essence of loneliness—the fear that one will never be able to find the word for what one desires to say. The word forms only in the darkest pools of one's being. The barest outline offers itself from the shadows. A monster is slain.

*'Twas brillig and the slithy toves did gyre and gimble
in the wabe.*

Dodgson lay down on the sofa, his knees curled up to his chest like a child. Maybe if he didn't try to go back to sleep, his body would be tricked. He could hear the reverberations of his pulse echoing through the pillow down. The pound-pound-pound disturbing him because it made him think of the inevitable break. The problem was that when he closed his eyes he could feel every ounce of his being fighting sleep. As if the feeling of oblivion overtaking his body was the real thing. The body is so fragile, bones, skin, heart, none of it amounts to much protection against harm. God has given us this soft, complicated, easily bruised container for our highest hopes; he has made us so fallible as to be comic, so vulnerable to age, and disease, to growths deep within our bodies, running through our blood. . . .

These were only more-sophisticated versions of the thoughts he'd had as a boy, every time he was alone in bed. They had gotten much worse at around the time his newborn sister died. He was ashamed to admit to himself that the primary effect her death had on him was fear. He was consumed by the idea that he, too, was going to be swept away in the middle of the night. And his father's words—*she passed, she was taken from us, Thy will be done*—did nothing to clear up the mystery and illuminate the facts. He was a religious man. These things were not talked of in a scientific manner. But his sister's death remained a diffuse threat hovering in the air like a damp night fog. *I pray the Lord my soul to keep. And if I die before I wake I pray the Lord my soul to take. . . .* He thought he might die in his sleep every time he closed his eyes.

Dodgson watched the sky make the slow transition from muddy black to lavender; he was always surprised that the sun rose even though you were watching. His whole body called out for sleep. But he knew from experience that trying and failing would only make him feel worse. The trick was to pretend nothing was wrong.

The light always looked dirty when you stayed up all night.

His mother's death was sudden. Inflammation of the brain, the doctors called it. Four months after arriving at Oxford, he had to turn around and go back for the funeral. He was nineteen. On the train home, the sky was the color of violets and ashes. He spread out his books and papers on the leather seat next to him and scribbled guiltily the entire way. Alternative methods of proving that parallel lines never meet. Were there any practical tests for the meeting of lines that could rival Euclid's? He had Euclid's 12th Axiom open on his lap. One of his favorites, so eloquent and moving in its way. Everything flows from it. *My Darling Charlie,* she wrote to him as a child. *I send you 1,000,000,000 kisses. Divide them in half and share them with your sisters please.* In proofs nothing is lost. Every factor is accounted for and conserved; every factor can be converted or shifted but never simply drifts out of the picture.

Dodgson could remember his mother holding him as a baby. Or was it just that he had seen her holding a baby so many times? No, he could remember her holding him, the sweet milk smell of her skin. Melting into her as if her freckled chest were part of him. His fingers in her sun-colored hair. *Charlie. Charlie.* The feeling of merging completely, hearing his cry from her mouth.

When he was seven there had been another funeral. He had not minded driving to the churchyard in a coach draped with black velvet. But once they got out there were relatives bending over, as if they were offering him a piece of candy, patting him, whispering, *Your sister is in heaven. Your sister has gone to God.* When did this baby have time to become his sister? To him, she was a newborn that had not been born. A birthday that had no birth. He was confused about the words that seemed to come detached from their meanings, that seemed to swing and dangle like trapdoors.

His sisters looked unfamiliar and adult in their black crepe dresses, the fabric too stiff and shiny to touch. There were tears running down their faces. But his mind was stubbornly literal. He was working on the problem. *Your sister has gone to God.* He thought of the plaid blanket neatly folded and flung over the side of the cradle.

He stood next to his father at the edge of the grave. He looked at him but his father's eyes were focused on the grave. The tiny casket, all gleaming braided gold and mahogany, was being lowered into the ground. Everyone watched, their heads bowed. But he was looking up to see if her soul escaped.

The truth is that he had not wanted this sister. A thought he tried to lose in the hymn. Let the words flood into his mind and drown it. *Divide them in half and share them with your sisters.* The night she was born he had taken his blanket and put it, wet and woolen, in his mouth. Soggy and sucked on. A baby again.

There engraved in fresh white cross-shaped stone: *Jesus called a little child unto Him.*

He remembered seeing the shovels of dirt fall on the bright mahogany of the coffin and then separate into grains. He remembered the white-pink lilies thrown there, with their pale, moist-looking stems.

Under his father's eyes were dark brown crescents. He said, *Your sister is an angel.* But even he, the Reverend of Daresbury, looked as if he were struggling to speak a foreign language that could not quite carry his meaning. Charles was trying to understand that we find ways of talking about things there are no ways of talking about. *Your sister is an angel.* The fear knotted in his chest was an "angel." Twelve years later, when his mother died, there was a pain in his stomach that clenched and seemed like it would go on clenching. The hole his mother left was an "angel."

The bewilderment stayed with him, only it had settled down and turned into something else. When he came up against a paradox, a logic problem that was impossible to solve or understand, he felt unaccountably at home. A sense of pleasure spreading through his chest. As if he has come to the place his mother is.

❦

The pattern of the cast-iron garden chair was pressing diamonds into Alice's thighs. She was watching Dodgson fold a piece of paper into a pistol. Under the bench Edith was teasing the kitten in the grass. It would make a bang, Dodgson promised. But who cared about pistols and bangs? Alice widened her eyes so that she could see the air, particles of static, vibrating blue, yellow, and white dots. She was annoyed with Dodgson for his meticulousness, for his long, thin fingers with perfectly oval nails, for the paper he had carried down from his rooms so neatly in a leather folder, all for her pleasure, she knew, but it embarrassed her, the trouble he had taken, the whole production. She felt uncomfortable, like it was her he was folding into small triangles.

A ladybug crawled along the back of her chair and Alice swung around and took it in her hand and felt it tickle her palm and watched it fly awkwardly off. She could feel Dodgson's accusation in the way he held himself so stiffly, pressing the folds with overly deliberate motions. It had been three weeks that they had been sitting there. Or so it felt. Just then Lorina slammed open the kitchen door and demanded that Alice look at the gray rock with specks of mica that friends of her parents had brought. Splendid, Alice said. Dodgson was folding without looking up. The rock was glittering in the sun. Alice sprinted, diamond-thighed, into the house.

Edith began to chatter, to fill the space where Alice had been with words. Had he ever thought of taking photographs of the cat? Did he want to go see the new snapdragons, such a lovely name, snapdragon, didn't he think? Edith was proud of her ability to make small talk with adults. Her mother said she knew how to draw people out.

Dodgson would not be drawn out.

The night before, entirely against her will, Edith had been

dressed in the same white muslin dress with lilac ribbons as Alice for their mother's dinner party. The guests beamed down at them, two large-eyed, ringleted girls in identical white dresses, and yet Edith was furious. Everything was cut in half and doubled and imitated until it meant nothing.

Dodgson was looking over her shoulder at the kitchen door.

Edith thought she remembered when Dodgson first started coming to the house even though she was only a baby. He seemed especially interested in her. He lifted her onto his lap, whispering rhymes into her ear, stroking her hair.

"Alice is certainly a favorite of our Mr. Dodgson," her mother had said lightly over tea several days before, and Edith felt the comment sharply as an insult. As if she had failed in the most important test life had thus far placed in her path. She felt like the time she was lost in a crowd at the train station. There wasn't enough air. Her mother was separated from her by the men and women, black legs and billowy skirts and suit-cases, swirling between them.

Of course Alice had a way of conquering everyone and everything. For instance, the cat. Dinah was originally sup-posed to be Ina's cat. There was really no ambiguity on this point, as Dinah had arrived on Ina's birthday with a blue satin bow around her neck. But then Alice took her, slowly and se-cretly, so that you couldn't point to the moment it happened; she made the cat love her, and follow her, and eat from her hand, and spent such an exhaustive amount of energy petting her and talking to her that soon, without even realizing they were doing it, the entire family referred to her as "Alice's cat."

"Shall we do some photographs, Mr. Dodgson?" Edith asked.

"I don't think so, Edith," he said absently. "Not this afternoon."

There was nothing Edith adored more than having her photograph taken. A few months earlier Mr. Dodgson had taken her into his rooms for the first time. He escorted her to the red divan with its swirling oriental plants. Next to it was a vase of bell-shaped flowers.

"May I pin up your sleeves, Edith?" he had asked her. He never called her Edie like everyone else. He called her Edith. And he treated her with a kind of physical deference that almost no adults of her acquaintance did, asking if he could pin up her dress without just going ahead without her permission. He went down on his knees, with pins in his mouth, and began working on the sleeves, until they were evenly pinned.

She was careful not to move. She was sure that she had moved less than Alice, less than the Macdonald girls, less than anyone who had come to his rooms to have their picture taken. Perfect, he told her from behind the camera. Beautiful. She had felt the seconds themselves breathe and expand, her throat dry, her lungs aching, but she did not breathe. Stay perfectly still, he said. Even though she wasn't smiling in any of the photographs, she thought Mr. Dodgson must have been impressed with her ability to follow directions.

"Let me take those out for you," he'd said when he was finished, gently removing the pins. And then she leaned back against the sofa, for one more picture.

Afterward he gave her ginger beer and biscuits.

But he hadn't invited her back.

The thing that particularly galled Edith was that she was prettier than Alice. She had overheard her mother saying so to her father. But still, she searched her reflection in the marble-framed mirror above her mother's washstand: the heart-shaped face, plump cheeks, the auburn curls her father loved to run his fingers through. She searched for a sign of what was missing. For what Mr. Dodgson didn't see.

He was sitting next to her in broody silence. She wanted to climb on his lap.

"You must excuse me, Edith," Mr. Dodgson said, getting up. She watched him duck under the low-hanging branch and walk away.

The older girls' voices floated down through an open win-dow, *nous voulons, vous voulez*, and then Miss Prickett's abominable accent. *Je voulais*. He could teach them French bet-ter than she could, but of course he could hardly propose him-self.

Il voudrait, elle voudrait, he could hear Alice now alone. He was charmed by the familiar voice wrapped around the for-eign syllables. Now they were moving on to another tense. Future. Imperfect. What if he and Alice lived in Paris alone in a flat with a garden, walking up the long, paint-chipped stair-way? Their rooms would have window boxes of sunflowers, and outside the large, shuttered windows, a country without kings.

He made his way slowly through the courtyard toward his rooms.

He opened his door, lay down his books, scanned the mail as he always did for a scallop-edged invitation, and finding none, began to prepare his usual meal. He made tea, allowing the leaves to soak for exactly four minutes, allowing it to cool for thirty seconds. And then he embarked on his meal of one poached egg and one piece of toast. There was no chance of his inadvertently eating two poached eggs or three pieces of toast. Dodgson relished precision and discipline the way someone else might relish a large dinner of roast duck and aubergines and sweet potatoes. He was particularly adept at controlling his appetite. He was not the sort to indulge.

After eating, he sat at his desk reviewing his Euclid dialogue, and when his thoughts traveled to the nagging of his stomach, to Alice, to the scruffy gray bird hopping through the vines outside his window, he called them back with no difficulty whatsoever. He had trained himself from childhood to focus intently on a single point of contemplation. This was part of why school was never difficult for him; long before he arrived there, he had mastered the art of not thinking about what was interesting him. At least until everyone else was asleep.

That night Dodgson lay under the sheets in his narrow bed, French verbs passing in front of his eyes like sheep. *Dormir. Dormais.* We are about to enter the future imperfect.

May 27, 1862
The dreams are worse. Last night we were on my
red sofa, but it was not faded & shabby as it is in life,
but richer crimson, plush & velvet & tufted & draped.
She lies like a tiny odalisque, her arms folded beneath
her head, her hair (somehow longer and curlier like

someone out of Dante Rossetti or Burne-Jones) flowing against a pillow, her small hips curving to the side, bones protruding. She smiles in a way I have never seen before. I lean down & kiss her gently on the forehead & it feels perfectly natural & harmonious as in a painting—& I start to touch her cheek & the reds & browns darken & her features shift—nose, mouth, eyes, sliding out of place—until her face is not perfect but monstrous. This is what I find so shattering about my dreams—they start out so pleasantly. I think if I had straightforward nightmares, I should find them less difficult. I should simply avoid sleep or wake relieved to see the hardwood floors and ceiling & a bit of sky out the window. What is most unnerving is how quickly the good dreams dissolve into bad, how blissful & wretched all at once, how I am swimming & swimming through them, & not at all sure which way I wish to come out— wake up?—go deeper in? These dreams in which terrible things happen also contain within them spots of greater joy and contentment than I have ever known in life— this is what confounds me—I wake muddled; sin & virtue, serenity & torment, thrown together & entwined until I barely know who I am.

The next morning Alice was furious at him. From the moment he walked in the door, a box of chocolate creams tucked under his arm, he could feel her anger. Vaguely, at first, as if the furniture had been shifted but he was not sure how. Mrs. Liddell stood beside him in the dark hallway. He could see the girls in the far corner of the drawing room on the gold sofa, its heavy wings spread out behind them. A chessboard perched on the table. His cheeks were burning. Alice's eyes remained fixed on the chess pieces. He searched through the past few days with scholarly thoroughness, going through every minor footnote of what happened (two games of backgammon, and one story, one brief hello in the garden) to see if there was any way he could possibly have offended her. But he came up with nothing. In fact when he had said good-bye two days earlier she had put her arms around his waist. He remembered it clearly. She was wearing a yellow dress with puffed sleeves. He hadn't seen her since. He looked at the lamp on the hall table. A brass man in a loincloth on his knees holding up a round orb of light. Not knowing what else to do, he handed Mrs. Liddell the chocolate creams he had brought for the girls.

"Thank you, Mr. Dodgson," she said. "How kind of you."

Alice's eyes flicked up at him briefly as if he were an inanimate object, an umbrella, a chandelier. He felt disemboweled, transparent. Reminding him of the day at school when the boys decided to refer to him as "it" and "thing" instead of "he" and "him." Ignore them, he told himself. But he could feel the metamorphosis. Its cheeks burned. The thing cowered.

Alice continued playing chess with Ina.

"Your move, Ina," she said, her voice sounding eerily adult—reproachful and mildly bored. The lady at the tea party.

He stood there, his hat in his hand, hesitating, ridiculous. Obviously not hiding his confusion.

"As you can see, the girls are quite absorbed in chess," said Mrs. Liddell gently. "Perhaps another time?"

Alice was staring at the pale gray veins in her marble knight. She hadn't wanted to ignore Dodgson. She blamed her older sister, who had taunted her about him the night before. The girls had been huddled under the covers in Ina's brass bed. They had stolen one of their mother's old penny dreadfuls, called *Wagner: the Wehr-Wolf*. Ina was reading the description of the beautiful murderess whose lover turned into a werewolf once a month: *She was attired in deep black; her luxuriant raven hair, no longer descending in shining curls, was gathered up in massy bands at the sides, and in a knot behind, whence hung a rich veil that meandered over her body's splendidly symmetrical length of limb in such a manner as to aid her attire in shaping rather than hiding the contours of that matchless form.*

On the next page she died tragically with great remorse.

Ina looked up from the story. "In spite of her splendidly symmetrical length of limb," she said theatrically, "Alice shall have to marry Mr. Dodgson."

"I am not marrying anyone," Alice said.

"She is not old enough," said Edith.

"He shall take beautiful photographs of your wedding."

"One can't take photographs of one's own wedding," Alice objected.

"But unfortunately your children will be rabbits and dwarves who s-s-s-stutter."

"May we go back to the book?" Alice rolled her eyes.

Lorina had decided that Mr. Dodgson was not a proper adult, and not one to be sought after and cultivated in spite of the obvious interest he showed in them. There was a lack of dignity in his willingness to kneel down on the ground, to get grass stains on his trousers, or in the drawings he brought as offerings, like flowers, trying to ingratiate himself to three little girls. Lorina much preferred the rhetoric reader, Mr. Joyce, with his wheat-straw hair and delft-blue eyes, and his tendency to talk to the elder Liddells without noticing her and her sisters.

"I would marry Mr. Dodgson," Edith offered.

"You will never be married," Alice said. "Keep reading."

Ina went on: *The voluptuous development of her bust was shrouded, not concealed, by the stomacher of black velvet which she wore, and which set off in strong relief the dazzling whiteness of her neck.*

That was their favorite part. Shrouded, not concealed.

And so Alice wanted to make a show of independence for Ina's sake. She wanted Ina to see how uninterested she was in Dodgson. At least that was how it started, but then she got caught up in it. She saw the confusion on Dodgson's face, but she couldn't stop. His face opened up to her. He looked hurt and then he tried to hide how hurt he was, which made him look even more hurt. A deep curiosity moved inside her. He was not like the hero of the story: *Those who would insult him shrunk abashed before the proud fire that shone from his eye, but in the drawing room, or the boudoir, whose eyes possessed more melting power, whose look more softness, whose glance more insinuation than his?* And yet here he was, a grown man in a waistcoat, whose unremarkable gray eyes filled with unhappiness because of her.

"Rook to pawn," she said coldly to Ina.

Ina's bishop was stalking her queen. Instead of turning and walking out the door, as she was afraid for a second he would,

Dodgson just stood there helplessly. He could not leave her; her indifference only pulled him further in, like a marionette on an invisible thread, made it more difficult for him to put on his hat and turn his back. She felt radiant, watching her actions move across his face like the weather. Her slightest mood magnified and reflected back to her. So this was the feeling of hurting a man, so awful and pleasurable at once. Alice had never felt it before.

8

June was hotter than usual. Even inside the deanery, the heat hung thick in the air. Mrs. Liddell looked up from her stitching—fluffy tree, jagged sky—at the young man sprawled out on her sofa. Charles Francis Needham, Viscount of Newry. His father had gone to school with her husband. His pale, almost clear blue eyes were surrounded by thick black eyelashes. He reminded her of the statues she had seen in Italy, curly-haired and perfect and slightly rounded like a woman.

"I've been invited to a house party at Lady Carbury's next week."

"How lovely," she said, pulling the needle through the sky.

"I suppose."

"Why shouldn't it be?"

"Twenty-six people trapped in a house with nothing to do but guzzle whiskey-and-water and worry about rain."

"I should think you would quite like that." She smiled. "The whiskey-and-water part, that is."

When she reached for a scissors on the side table, he saw a strip of petticoat, a camel-colored boot with buttons up the side. She straightened her dress.

"If you must know I'm hard at work," he said. "On a play."

"Oh?" she said, knotting the yarn.

His skin was the color of milky tea. Skin like that was the best argument against Darwin she could think of, physical proof of a divine plan. The real *Origin of Species* and smooth, milky skin. But somehow all of these beautiful boys became so ordinary. She remembered when Henry used to walk into a room, every woman in it felt his presence. The electric rustle of air, the rearranging of a room to make space. And now he was still handsome in a distinguished dean sort of way, but diminished, lined, balded as if life had wrung through him. Was that fair? Not entirely, but once you commit yourself to a certain path, a certain life with someone, then all of the possibilities you have lost start to appear on your face, to carve their paths.

Lord Newry stretched out his legs, his hands in his pockets. He leaned back and looked up at the ceiling. He had light stubble on his chin. She felt strange, felt her position, wife, mother, embroiderer, coming undone, unraveling in the heat. All the young men she had met before she was married came back to her, the possibilities lined up like green railway novels on the shelf next to her bed: *Confessions of a Pretty Woman* and *The Banker's Wife* and *Peers and Parvenus*.

She had gone to all the dances along with the other eligible girls in her set. The choices seemed to glide through a room, the core of who she was spinning and changing shape with every partner. There was the Greys' soaring ballroom, with the oval gilt mirror above the fireplace, there was the Smiths' dining room, with twisted gold candlesticks on the table, there was the Bascombes' lawn, the tables lit up with lanterns. It seemed so random, who she ended up dancing with, the pressure of a hand on the small of her back. And then there was the strange thought she had during one of the crushes thrown by her next-door neighbors: *it didn't matter who she danced with.* She suspected the same might have been true of marriage. No matter which of the men she had selected, when she stumbled out with him onto the lawn, his breath white from the cold, his silhouette barely visible in the darkness, the conversation about Shelley, or the dogs on his estate, or where he had his suits made, it would not have been different.

The balls of green and yellow yarn lay at her feet. She picked up the yellow and began untangling it.

"Any interesting young women?" she said, motherly again.

"No one interesting *and* pretty."

She allowed the silence to settle over them, her fingers occupied with the yarn.

Then she said abruptly, "How is the Greek coming along?"

Her hands moved to her stomach. She was going to have another baby. She could feel it.

Alice was curled up next to him, the candle throwing barely enough light to read. The smell of roasting duck for the twenty-person dinner party below drifted up the stairs. William Thackeray had been invited, along with several lesser-known critics and poets. A literary evening, Mrs. Liddell had whispered in his ear while the servant was taking his coat. Dodgson slipped up to the nursery before the guests were called in to dinner. To say good night. Now he was reading her a poem he had made up: *When on the sandy shore I sit, beside the sea-salt wave, and falling into a weeping fit, because I dare not shave.* She was falling asleep but trying to stay awake for him, fighting it off for him. She looked smaller, folded against him.

"Off to bed, Alice!" Mrs. Liddell called from the stairs. "Off to bed!"

Dodgson felt her warmth through her thin nightgown. His arm circled her back, his hand resting lightly on her hip, her hair falling on his sleeve. She seemed to be asleep. Her finger in her mouth. The rhythm of her breathing merged with his.

Mrs. Liddell said, a little louder now: "Off to bed!"

"Off with her head," Dodgson whispered to himself. "Off with her head."

Alice smiled.

Dodgson reached for Richardson's *Clarissa* immediately upon returning home. He had taken it out of the library in a moment of idle curiosity. How could thousands of readers make it through such a dauntingly long tragedy about one woman's ruin? The title page read:

Clarissa, Or the History of a Young Lady:
Comprehending *the most* Important Concerns *of*

Private Life, and particularly showing the DISTRESSES that may attend the Misconduct both of PARENTS and CHILDREN in Relation to MARRIAGE.

He stretched out on the divan with the 1,100-page book, and he came across the line, "She was never left out of a party of pleasure after she had passed her ninth year." He read it again. Nine? Wasn't that young for parties of pleasure? Somehow the "of pleasure" made it sound even worse. Of course, that was the 1750s. But then most girls, even now, were raised differently than his sisters, especially when their parents had high marital aspirations for them. They were taken out into the world all wrapped in pink and purple silk sashes, like premature little buds in late February. White kid gloves. Daisies in their hair. They were trained early in the arts of . . . Dodgson closed the book and put it on the floor. Alice was ten.

July 4, 1862

Had a hideous visitation this morning—I looked in the glass and saw a bedraggled creature rising toward me, pale & greenish, with a piggish nose, hooded eyes & the lines of an entire street map of London carved into its face. It comes at one with an ugliness that startles— the self delivered monstrous & grossly physical.

When I arrived at the deanery, still shaken from the morning's apparition, the girls were putting on their hats. Duckworth & I were taking them on a longer boat expedition than usual, all the way to Godstow. We made our way to Folly Bridge at eight o'clock & by the time we loaded up the boat we could already feel the heat. I pulled the safety pins out of my lapel & sat on the dock with pins in my mouth & began pinning the hems of the girls' skirts.

As we drifted, I began a tale about Alice falling down a rabbit hole, seeing cupboards and jars of marmalade as she fell. The children were mesmerized, the gentle glide of the boat, the beating sun, the sound of my voice, and oars hitting water, the hum of river insects, seemed to have an almost hypnotic effect.

What a curious feeling, said my invented Alice. I must be shutting up like a telescope.

Dodgson, is this an extempore romance of yours? asked Duckworth.

I was hardly aware of what I was saying. The story was moving past me, carrying me like the water itself.

What was Alice wearing? interrupted Edith.

A cotton dress, I answered. Blue.

For a moment, I thought of the boat tipping over & everyone except Alice sinking slowly into the river.

Later we lay in the shade under the haycocks, Alice inches away from me on the grass, a layer of stickiness on her face, wetting the hair that fell across her forehead. She stretched out her legs. In the distance, we could see the top of Lorina's and Duckworth's heads bobbing up & down. They were walking by the riverbank, looking for stones.

Alice was fanning her legs with her dress & the words came faster—how can one describe it?—at once maddening & exhilarating—the words flying past my

understanding & forming themselves into story—
Creatures storming my mind—Words coming unpried
from their meanings & spinning through bright air—

The only frustration was Edith, who kept interrupt-
ing. Wait I don't like this part. What does the pigeon
mean when he says "all little girls are serpents"?

I explained patiently: Only that little girls eat eggs
& serpents eat eggs & therefore little girls are serpents.

I don't like that part, she said again.

The sky was a clear blue, the heat thick. We rowed
home, me in my white flannel trousers and straw hat,
our half-eaten picnic of strawberries and cold chicken
sandwiches and cakes still there, beneath the back bench
in the picnic basket. As the bridge came into view, the
mock turtle starts singing "Will you won't you? Will
you won't you? Won't you join the dance?" Alice sat
next to me. She pulled off her shoes.

We passed under an overhanging branch. It blocked
out the sun for a moment. Suddenly I saw a disturbing
artifice in her smile—a tilt of her head—a shadow of
the woman she would become passing across her face—
perfumed & high-heeled & posing. Time is running out.
The white rabbit with pink eyes & pocket watch & top
hat, very handsomely dressed, hurries by, "I am late. I
am late." Alice laughed. Edith & Ina laughed & the
three of them couldn't stop laughing & giggling & it
buoyed me & carried me up, soothing the panic I was
feeling a moment before. We are just children & rabbits.
For the time being.

When they got to the shore Alice was anxious. Everybody else was elated. But Alice was anxious. She memorized parts of the story as he was telling it but she wanted it written down, his handwriting on the page making it homemade and manageable. Dodgson was strange that afternoon and not quite himself. Better than himself. But not quite himself.

He was fiddling with the rope. She was unpinning her skirt. His attention was focused on her but somewhere inside that focus she felt his impatience. He was moving away from her in nervous eddies, like river water over black stone. She wasn't sure how she felt about the story. She certainly didn't like the part where she was growing in the house, pushing against the walls, her shoulders cramped, her chin digging into her chest, her head banging against the ceiling, her large, swelling self boxed in and crumpled and pent up. She didn't like the part where he says her neck is almost broken. Or where Alice says, *But then shall I never get older than I am now? That'll be a comfort one way—never to be an old woman.*

She felt in the story a threat. It was somehow more personal than the rhymes he recited for her in the nursery. The story was like a letter he was writing in code, which was something he often did. (The last one read: *tseraeD ecilA, I ma kcuts ni a rorrim. EsealP pleh em. sruoY yletanoitceffA, selrahC nosgdoD.* "Mr. Nose-god," she had called him for weeks afterward). But that was what he did. He sent letters you had to hold up to a mirror. Letters you had to read with a magnifying glass. Letters made up of small pictures. Letters that made you feel that no one else could read them even if they tried. Only your cleverness, your unique quality of mind, could turn the nonsensical scribblings into alphabetical coherency. There was the flutter of fear that you wouldn't understand them and then the relief when you did. And then the lingering sense, when you'd actually written out the translation, that there was something else there, still hidden.

Alice loved the story because she was afraid of the story. She found it pleasurable, the way the moment you wake up from a particularly frightening dream and see the familiar blue flowers that look like birds in the wallpaper of the bedroom you've slept in all your life is pleasurable; it was that pleasure she found in the story, the pleasure of return.

So Alice asked him, the long grass tickling her bare calves, the dirt wet under her feet, to write down everything he said on the boat ride. She wanted it now, to hold in her hands. Hers was the same impulse that leads engaged women to want jewels—bright testaments to undying emotion—at precisely the moment when everything is in flux. But Alice was a child. And she wanted the story. Written down.

Dodgson was in his straw hat tying the boat to the small dock, keeping one foot on the boat so it wouldn't drift away in the current and one foot on the bank, when Alice, standing several feet away on the shore, started begging him to write the story down for her.

The water was glassy and green. He was concentrating on the knot. He felt the water sliding in his shoes. He felt the dampness in his trousers hitting his legs. Write it down? He couldn't think of anything worse. In fact, it bothered him that she had even asked him. The story was part of the boat ride, the characters left in the trees, scattered through the day, hanging in the air, not something to be made solid. He thought she of all people would understand that. The story was meant to be like the Cheshire cat, perching on a branch, then slowly vanishing, leaving only a grin. But she was looking at him, shielding her eyes from the sun, and he found it difficult to say no to her. Please, she begged. It was so rare that she begged him for anything that he couldn't resist. So he offered a string of vague affirmatives: Perhaps. Yes. We'll see.

The whole trip already felt like too much to him, too much given away, too much nearly lost. He was tired. His back hurt from rowing. The sun was low and red, the trees burnt orange, singed with brown, and he suddenly wanted to be home, on his divan, stretching out, thinking up syllogisms for his lecture the next morning.

But by the time he unlocked his door, he had convinced himself that the afternoon was perfect. That was one of his talents. He managed to convert life into happy memories almost as it was happening. A kind of instant nostalgia. He forgot his fierce desire to capsize the boat, so that he was alone with Alice, and everyone else fell headfirst into the water; he forgot the uneasiness he felt when Alice demanded that he write down the story. Memory famously has this effect, a selective editing out of the more disturbing parts of life, but with Dodgson it wasn't memory; it was experience itself. This capacity, this instant mental cleansing, allowed him to isolate the moment, to take out its more enjoyable elements and throw away the rest. So that he was left with what he later referred to as "that golden afternoon."

Dodgson noted down "the cloudless blue above, the watery

mirror below." He commented frequently on the cloudlessness and perfection of the day. However, the London Meteorological Society recorded the weather around Oxford on July 4, 1862, as "rather cool and wet." Dodgson's capacity for instant nostalgia affected even the weather. But it wasn't the instinctive whitewashing of the times, the sentimental looking backward; by the time he walked into his rooms, that pure goldenness was simply how he experienced the afternoon—it really *was* cloudless blue.

9

The dean closed his eyes. The dons were boring him. When he couldn't get what he wanted he quickly got bored, moving on to the next thing, making up for lost time before it was lost. He was plotting a dinner with John Ruskin to discuss the possibility of bringing Dante Gabriel Rossetti, Edward Burne-Jones, William Morris, and the rest back to Oxford to paint murals on the interior of the museum. After dinner he would pour a glass of port (he would take out the '20) and they would step out into the garden (stars, velvet sky) and he would throw out the idea as if it had just occurred to him. The Morte D'Arthur mosaics had drawn a great deal of attention to the Union, and he thought perhaps if the same group did the museum . . . Bits of the dons' argument drifted up to the aqua blue fresco he was imagining. *Compromised the academic standards.* Tangles of red-blond hair floating as if in water. *Champagne parties that last until dawn.* Perhaps a scene from the Bible would be best, if he could convince them it was fashionable enough, or scenes from the life of Queen Elizabeth. *And then he was sick in the shrubs outside my room.* He drained the last sip from his glass.

Dean Liddell had invited his faculty—Mr. Clerke, Mr. Gordon, Mr. Prout, Mr. Sandford, Mr. Joyce, Mr. Bayne, Mr. Pickard, and Mr. Dodgson—over for an informal meeting to sort through a small bureaucratic tangle. His wife's protégé, Lord Newry, was applying for special permission to give a ball in Christ Church that would extend beyond the permitted hours, and he had gathered the night before that it was quite crucial to his wife's happiness that permission should be granted. He thought a good single-malt whiskey would smooth over the issue, though that was proving to be wrong.

The dean turned to Dodgson. "It's a mere half hour we're quibbling over."

"We've agreed before," Dodgson said. "Once we begin to officially sanction these sorts of—"

"We do occasionally break some of the more harmless rules ourselves," Sandford, the Greek reader, pointed out.

"To whom are you referring?"

"There was Buckland, for one," Sandford said.

Dr. William Buckland was the legendary geologist and mineralogist who lived in the corner of the great quadrangle. He kept bears, rats, jackals, snakes, rabbits, dogs, cats, and an entire menagerie, and served them as food to his guests, claiming he was eating his way through the animal kingdom.

"To the best of my knowledge," said Dodgson, smiling, "there aren't any rules governing culinary taste."

The dean filled Bayne's glass. He walked around the back of Dodgson's chair and refilled his. He found it odd that this man who whispered puns to his children, laced mathematical treatises with riddles, dined with wild-haired poets, and traipsed off to London for artists' soirees, should reserve all of his seriousness in life for a few extra hours of a party. But Dodgson was hard to fathom. At first he had thought the young mathematician and photographer might be an ally, a reformer, an architect of a different world. But he had quickly come up against his stubborn attachment to the rules, his fierce loyalty to the way things had always been. The dean also found it almost impossible to carry on a conversation with him. There was a resistance knotted up in Dodgson, an unwillingness to be drawn out. He lived too much in his own mind. Such a strange thing, a man alone. The dean thought of his own abundance, the servants making coffee in the kitchen, his wife reading in bed, his daughters running through the hallway, the new cradle waiting to be filled.

The dean surveyed his men around the table and planned his final siege. Joyce would be wanting dinner. Bayne, the classical tutor, almost always agreed with the dean, and Sandford and Clerke almost always went along with Bayne.

"It does seem like a bit too much fuss over a party," he said, looking at Bayne and Joyce, the rhetoric reader. "I should think we could turn our heads this once and be done with it."

"I quite agree," Joyce said. "Wasn't it Epicurus who said, pleasure is the beginning and the goal of a happy life?"

"And wasn't it Seneca who said, what need is there to weep over parts of life? The whole of it calls for tears." Dodgson was enjoying himself.

Bayne took his pocket watch out of his side pocket, a gesture the dean noted with interest. He knew that time was his strongest opposition; everyone wanted to be done with it, and Dodgson wasn't going to back down easily.

"It's true that if we allow him to carry on his party past the officially designated hour," said Joyce, "there will be others."

"In droves," agreed Bayne.

And it seemed to the dean's tremendous annoyance, eyeing two empty bottles of rather expensive whiskey, that with Greek, Latin, mathematics, and rhetoric against him, the matter was settled.

The other guests swarmed into the warm evening, but Dodgson hung back. He stood outside the deanery in the stillness. The walls were soaked purple. The soft sounds of clanging pots and servants' laughter floated through the window. And then it came to him, the large three-story red brick house, the pear trees on the edge of the lawn, the trellis with bell-shaped flowers poking through, the nursery with sloping ceiling, the library downstairs, the house he would never live in. It almost never happened that he saw his life from this particular angle, in this particular light: as a house he didn't have.

He had chosen this: narrow bed, tiny japanned sponge bath, low bookshelves with glass doors, white oceaned globe on brass stand, purple Turkish rug. He had chosen small crowded rooms attached to other small crowded rooms, had chosen even the idea of spreading a whole life into a few rooms. Like a student who had stayed, who had failed to move on. In fact there had been no choice. There was only blind drift. The current that pulled. The only life that fit.

Other people had other things; he had numbers, numbness.

It is strange to be a prisoner who has designed your own cell. The architecture of your unhappiness. The stone walls you have dreamt up. The bars you have desired. The spikes and spires you have created. You wouldn't have it any other way. The longing for the outside becomes more complicated for this sort of prisoner. The outside is—nicked moon hanging low, cool air through curling leaves—what you never wanted. What you were keeping out.

Dodgson lay in his bed, shut up like a telescope.

Almost never did he feel it, the panic of loneliness, like a flock of birds taking flight in his chest.

What more could he want. A mind that moves with his.

The next morning Dodgson was passing through the Great Hall with its high vaulted ceilings and stained-glass windows. Students were scattered everywhere, reading and talking and napping. Dodgson's eye was drawn to the headlines of a *Gazette* someone had abandoned on one of the heavy wooden tables. The front-page story was an exposé about girls of ten or eleven being sold to depraved gentlemen for a few shillings. It emerged in five long columns of newsprint that in these houses of disrepute, in the worst neighborhoods of London, the girls were chloroformed until they lay lifeless on a bed. And then "unspeakable acts" were perpetrated on them. He flushed. He looked up at the students in their robes strolling past in twos and threes. He imagined that they were reading the two-inch headline—INNOCENCE LOST!—and looking at him. And this was a respectable paper. Dodgson folded the paper and tucked it under his arm and hurried down the hall.

Dodgson made his way through the hallway and up the stairs into his rooms. He read all the way through the article while standing up in the foyer outside his door.

He could not quite bring himself to throw the paper out—after all, the scout might read it if he were to place it in the rubbish. He settled on hiding it under the bottom cushion of his sofa. He would decide how to dispose of it later.

He couldn't stop the pictures of a shabby girlchild in an overbright room. He thought of sweet chloroform filling her lungs and washing through her head an artificial peace. He saw her go limp, as an unnamed gentleman watched. And then he saw a row of doors along the hallway with other girls inside the rooms in various states of drugged acquiescence. He saw it as clearly as if the article had been accompanied by photographs. A line from his own story ran inexplicably through his head: *All little girls are serpents*. He decided to write a letter to the editors. The outrage came pouring out of his pen: "I plead for our young men and boys, whose imaginations are being excited by highly colored pictures of vice. . . . I plead for our pure maidens whose souls are being saddened, if not defiled by the nauseous literature that is thus thrust upon them. . . ." The idea of an underworld where hidden desires, the stuff of nightmares and fantasies, could be consummated with impunity for a few shillings filled Dodgson with horror. He particularly objected to the idea of that consummation being exploited in newsprint. He thought it was corrupting, to spell it out. As always, Dodgson wished the underground to remain underground.

⚜

Hunt and Dodgson were sitting at the round rosewood table by the window, a chessboard between them.

"Finally, a game that rewards the quiet and contemplative," Dodgson said, moving his rook.

Hunt stared at the board and pushed his queen diagonally. "The meek shall inherit the earth, is it?"

Dodgson found it hard to look at Hunt in this new place, new for the two of them. He had never invited Hunt to his rooms before. When he first opened the door, he was startled by Hunt's physical presence. As if by a bird flying out of a cage, the chaotic flapping of wings. Hunt was tall. His mouth large and vulnerable. His shoulders stooped. His trousers frayed. Dodgson felt like he was seeing him for the first time. Luckily they had the game.

Rarely did Dodgson find anyone with whom he was interested in playing chess. His mind moved the pieces according to what could happen, following the complicated lacing of paths, the thick net of possibilities hovering above the board. That was the pleasure of chess for him, the layers of thought that existed simultaneously. Hunt played the same way.

"Tell me about the Newry imbroglio I've been hearing so much about."

"What should you like to know?"

"What was it you found so objectionable about the ball?"

"It is my belief." Dodgson looked up from the board. "That

there are certain traditions that should be upheld and respected."

"And if they aren't upheld and respected?"

"Then," Dodgson began. "We are no better than—"

"What?" Hunt asked, taking his pawn.

Dodgson saw five moves ahead. Hunt was trapping him with the pawn and bishop. He said nothing. He felt the tension between the sandalwood pieces, felt the difficulty of holding the game in his head. He found the mental exhaustion relaxing. He felt something opening up between him and Hunt, something he would not presume to call friendship. But he felt a sudden pleasure in Hunt's company that was new.

"You still haven't quite explained."

"It's hardly mysterious. I simply believe the young should be protected."

"From what?"

"From themselves," Dodgson said. "Amongst other things."

"But surely you don't believe you can protect anyone from themselves," Hunt said. "No matter how many balls you forbid."

"We didn't forbid it," Dodgson said. "We simply refrained from making an exception to a previously existing rule. Preventing an unseemly spectacle."

"Unseemly?" Hunt said. "It seems quite the opposite to me. Import a little beauty to the gray old place. What is the worst that could happen?"

The question surprised Dodgson. *The worst that could happen.* It engaged him like the chessboard. Imagine the worst and then imagine it happening. His mind moved through. The music swelling through the courtyard. The naked shoulders. The dancing. The sweet, still grass the next morning. The pink haze lifting over stone . . . Perhaps Hunt was right. Nothing would be changed.

"Sometimes," said Hunt, "you sound more like the venerable archdeacon than his artistic son."

Dodgson made his move. Three squares forward. He looked up from the board.

"You could be right," he said, smiling, "and checkmate."

Out the window, the branches were washed in a dark apricot glow. The two men sat in companionable silence. Dodgson had not stuttered once.

10

Mrs. Liddell was serving breakfast to Mrs. Jasper and Mrs. Lamb at the cast-iron table in the far corner of the garden. The trees were yellow. The warm September wind rustled crisp leaves. She put her hands protectively over her swelling stomach. The maid carried the sausages and eggs and kidney pies from the kitchen on a silver tray. *A picnic breakfast,* she had scribbled on the invitation. A festive gesture to hide the fact that she did not particularly like either of her guests. They were her husband's colleagues' wives and she was compelled to entertain them.

"Have you seen the article about the opium den in Ratcliff Highway, the one Dickens visited?" asked Mrs. Jasper. She was a moon-faced woman with small black eyes.

"Oh, yes," Mrs. Liddell said, spooning the steaming eggs

from the silver tureen. "I had Henry bring it to me right away. How did you find it?"

"It was quite anticlimactic, I thought," Mrs. Jasper said, taking her plate. "And not terribly interesting."

"Yes, I was expecting something far more sordid," said Mrs. Lamb.

"Everyone seemed to be asleep."

"And it was quite immaculate."

"Though I did like the bit about the Chinaman. What was he called? Mr. Chang?"

The plate of sausages was almost empty. Mrs. Liddell was glad she had put out the good china with blue and pink roses.

"I stopped at the dressmaker yesterday," Mrs. Lamb said. "She has a lovely magenta silk."

"I should really have a dress made for Lorina's fourteenth birthday," Mrs. Liddell said.

Across the garden she saw Mr. Dodgson and Alice on the swing. She had the feeling that there was someplace else Alice was supposed to be but she could not think where.

"I find it difficult to believe they send their journalists out to smoke opium," said Mrs. Jasper. "Quite an occupation. Do you remember Mrs. Carville? Her niece is marrying a journalist."

"I'm not sure this particular shade would suit Lorina," said Mrs. Lamb. "Perhaps something brighter."

"Yes," said Mrs. Liddell vaguely.

She noticed Dodgson's arm draped over the back of the swing. Her eyes stopped on her daughter. Alice in her pale blue dress looked changed. She had trouble defining where the difference came in, a subtle change in attitude, perhaps, a new fullness in the face and shoulders. But this happened to girls; Mrs. Liddell remembered it happening to Lorina, one day when stick-thinness became grace.

"Did they have anything new besides the magenta?" Mrs. Jasper asked.

The smell of sausage drifted across the table; Mrs. Liddell felt queasy.

"They did have a nice green." Mrs. Liddell forced herself to turn back to her guests. "Though I'm not sure it's as fashionable."

The motion of the swing, back and forth, back and forth, seemed to catch in her head. It distracted her from the conversation, setting its own rhythm and sway.

"Have either of you been following the new Trollope?" Mrs. Liddell heard herself saying. "I am quite desperate to read the next installment."

"I shall never understood how anyone can plow through him," Mrs. Lamb said. "It's all bishops and politics."

"Lovely sausages," said Mrs. Jasper, reaching for the last one.

Mrs. Lamb glanced over at Dodgson and Alice.

"Our Mr. Dodgson is an excellent photographer," Mrs. Liddell said.

"Oh, yes," said Mrs. Jasper. "Everybody says so."

"Alice looks quite grown up," said Mrs. Lamb.

Mrs. Liddell looked over at her daughter, slowly absorbing the comment. Quite grown up.

The perfectly ordinary sight of Mr. Dodgson and Alice on the swing suddenly came at her more vividly, and in brighter color. Suddenly, in her head, they soared into a different place.

Alice had small swells of breasts hidden in the cotton drape of her dress with its childishly round collar, but not entirely. When you live with someone you do not see the small changes, but it now came to her that Alice had started hunching her shoulders, as if to hide the pulling fabric of her dress. Her shoulders and neck looked less boyish, softer. Back and forth, back and forth, it swung in and out of focus, the thing her mind was trying to comprehend: the sharp black outline of Dodgson and her pale blue daughter against the intricate lights and darks of the hedge. His arm resting along the back of the swing. Her head against his arm. Him leaning over to whisper something in her ear.

"My husband seems to do nothing but politics these days," she said, trying to recover herself.

"Yes," said Mrs. Jasper. "Isn't the entrance to the cathedral the latest controversy? I must say I cannot understand all the alliances and scheming."

"It makes them feel important," said Mrs. Lamb. "Like parliament itself meeting over a few feet of wood paneling."

A cloud passed in front of the sun. Mrs. Liddell straightened the napkin on her lap.

Something should be done, she thought. Something should have been done.

The maid came with the orange sponge cake. Mrs. Jasper took a large piece, balancing it with her fingers on the serving knife, and then served the others.

Mrs. Liddell felt the buttery cake dissolve in her mouth and thought suddenly of the mother in *The Banker's Wife: Her next resting place was the grave.*

"I've forgotten to tell you," said Mrs. Jasper. "My husband has promised me a trip to Italy in the spring."

"How blissful," said Mrs. Lamb.

Mrs. Liddell was distracted by an image of her husband's hand on hers, in a open air café in the Piazza San Marco, the pigeons flying from the church dome.

Alice's and Dodgson's heads rose up and the scene in front of her swung out of focus. Against the clear sky she saw: Alice kicking her legs. Dodgson leaning back. Orange trumpet vines spilling over the doorway. Ivy rippling in the breeze. An old friend of the family playing with a child on a sunny day. She put her hands around the swell of her stomach. The warmth of the day flowed through her. The reassuring smell of tea rose from the table.

"And then," said Dodgson, "there was the white rabbit looking at his pocket watch saying, I'm late, I'm late—"

"But," Alice interrupted. "How can they breathe underground?"

"It's quite interesting," he explained. "There is a thin slice of sky in the tunnel. It's an entire world, just like ours, but sunk under a layer of earth. Does that make sense?"

"Yes of course."

She thought for a moment. "What about the dodo? Is he real or did you invent him as well?"

"He was real. But he isn't anymore."

"How do you mean?"

"The last dodo died a hundred years ago."

"Could it fly?"

"I am afraid the dodo was one of the few birds on earth not graced with that particular gift."

Across the garden, Dodgson could see Mrs. Liddell and her friends seated around a table with a white tablecloth.

Alice said suddenly, "Are we going to get married?"

Dodgson froze for a moment. He reminded himself: children grow out of words as quickly as they grow out of clothes.

"Here's a riddle," he said. "The beginning of eternity, the end of time and space, the beginning of every end, and the end of every place?"

"That's a difficult one," Alice said. "Give me a minute."

He pushed the swing with his legs. He saw the faith in her features themselves: the faith that whatever happened would turn out properly; the feeling that everything would be taken care of, because it always was. Children live in happy endings, and it makes them luminous and smooth. They never think that they may not fall in love, or that they may be unhappy when they do, or that they may feel more abjectly alone with someone else than they did by themselves, or that they may spend the rest of their lives by themselves, because that was not the story they were told.

Her hair flew into her mouth. She brushed it away and turned toward him.

"Is it the letter e?"

"Of course. How clever of you to get it so quickly."

She jumped abruptly off the swing and ran inside.

The thought seared through him. He *could* marry Alice. He could go over to the deanery that evening and ask to see

Mr. Liddell and propose quite seriously that he should be engaged to Alice after she came of age, which was only a little over a year from now, after her twelfth birthday. They would wait several years, which was not unheard of. True, he was not one of the long-lashed lords who couldn't master basic algebra that Mrs. Liddell had her eye on, but still. He had means and lived close by.

He wound his way home, stopping at the pool in the middle of Tom Quad. Brown leaves swirled on the surface. And he had the odd feeling that he was considering the fate of a distant cousin he knew fairly well and liked.

That evening the brief fantasy warmed up his rooms like a fire: Alice lying in bed. Alice packing sandwiches to eat by the river. Alice in a white nightgown running through his rooms, Alice lying on the crimson sofa with her bare feet resting on the mahogany arm, Alice waking up next to him . . . He would sleep differently with her. He knew he would.

But no matter how much he expanded his mind, he could not imagine Alice older. Like a photograph that failed. A white star emanating from the center and spoiling the image. He could not see her face. She kept darting, running, and pulling away, his woodland animal. He could only picture her now. Ten and a half.

❧

Dodgson rushed out to get the latest issue of *Cornhill Magazine* so that he could read the new installment of *The Small House at Allington*. He was embarrassed by how eager he was to obtain it. But each section tantalized and pulled him further in, though nothing ever happened. Lily Dale continued to remain irrationally faithful to Crosbie, who had betrayed her, broken off their engagement, and run off with a lady of higher rank; and she continued to refuse handsome Johnny Eames, whom she was in fact quite attached to.

The story was one long reflection on perversity stretching out over months, each installment like another pearl on the string. Would she change her mind? Why wouldn't she change her mind? Dodgson found it strange that he was so caught up in this story that was not a story. This exercise in frustration, like a child practicing scales. The atmosphere of the novel was like a swamp, the air thick and warm, with pockets of flies; that same lack of motion, of vista; the feeling more of getting stuck than of reading.

So why did he open the magazine with such anticipation? Lily Dale was pushing ahead with a love that no one could understand, that led like a dead-end road to the barren seaside, a few brushes of grass in the dunes—in other words, to no city where anyone else lived—she could not live an ordinary life, could not build a house, in that love.

And then of course, no one in Trollope seemed to possess the purity of mind and heart one associated with the heroes and heroines of great literature. Even the ideal suitor Johnny Eames, dangled in front of the reader as the man Lily was supposed to marry, the good-hearted loyal John, had involved himself with another woman in his rooming house. The innocent were not innocent. The good were weak. Everyone in Trollope had complicated pasts and layers of attachment and peculiarities of affection. His characters refused the work of a novel: making themselves happy. That was the secret of Trollope, so unlike Austen, Thackeray, Dickens, or any other writer Dodgson had thus far encountered. Why this dark view of human character should be so soothing, he had no idea. But somehow *Small House* burst through him and gave him peace.

The story was so long and tedious that it held up a mirror to its devoted readers: why did they want Lily Dale to get married to Johnny Eames so desperately? Was it possible that she was better off alone? Were there complexities of feeling that could not be contained by the usual vows? The book forced the assumptions of the Mrs. Liddells of the world to crack open and reveal themselves for what they were: the easy, shallow, unthinking embrace of holy matrimony.

⚜

The man was older, with reddish side whiskers and brilliantly blue eyes. He was flamboyantly dressed in a greatcoat with a brown velvet collar and a bright blue neckcloth. Legendary art critic and creator of tastes. The man who had long ago persuaded Dodgson that he had no talent for drawing. Dodgson had been about to open the gate to the deanery when he saw them. But what on earth was John Ruskin doing playing croquet with Alice? He was stooping down to hit the ball with a mallet. His hat was balanced on the garden bench, next to a stack of loose papers under a stone. How strange that the eminent scholar would condescend to play games. Hadn't Ruskin railed against sport of all kind, the idle hitting of balls, and slashing of water with oars?

Dodgson hurried up the stairs to the library. He was technically the sublibrarian and therefore had the key to all the small rooms. He leaned his head against the window that offered the clearest view of the dean's garden. The stops and starts of the game told him they were talking. Dodgson knew Ruskin was distantly friendly with the dean, they had been at Christ Church together, but he did not know this friendship was sufficiently warm to include the family in its penumbra.

The way Alice was standing, her whole body tilting up toward the giant art critic, was making him furious. The arch of her back, her hands on her hips. Of course, Dodgson believed that little girls were paragons of innocence, trailing clouds of glory, as the Romantics thought, in other words, straight from God. He agreed with Dr. William Acton, the renowned medical expert on matters of the flesh, who wrote: "With healthy and well brought up children, no sexual notion or feeling has ever entered their heads, even in the way of speculation." But the way Alice was standing. That was the way she stood with *him*.

But what was Ruskin saying to her? Could he be lecturing her about the oppression of the working class? That's what he was doing the last time Dodgson overheard him. Ruskin was at the Liddells', his extraordinary blue eyes lit up and glittery from sherry, a thick ring of admirers surrounding him. Jealousy tore through Dodgson. Could Ruskin be plotting a proposal, the famous and well-published art critic and the very young daughter of the dean? He watched Alice lift the pink mallet above her shoulders. That overly emphatic swing.

Dodgson knew the bare outlines of Ruskin's romantic history. Everyone did. And even from two floors above he saw clearly the solicitousness in Ruskin's manner, saw from his posture that Ruskin had none of the feigned interest most adults show toward children. His tall body bent toward the tiny figure, rapt and cowed at once. Dodgson had the unnerving feeling, as he looked out the open window, that he was looking down from the boat into the river, seeing a reflection of himself, broken, distorted, shimmering, but himself nonetheless.

Twenty years earlier, John Ruskin had loved another child, Miss Euphemia Gray. Ruskin had known Effie for years, as the daughter of a friend of the family. He saw her at a dinner party at his parents' large brick house at 26 Herne Hill, when she was twelve. She was a dark-haired, gray-eyed slip of a thing with a precocious tendency to flirt. And he was the kind of man who turned relationships into little religions. So he had doted on her, as an angel, a bit of divine beauty fallen to earth. He applied all of his training as an art critic to her face, analyzing, studying and sketching it. He wrote to her, "It seems so like a dream—so impossible—that I should be loved." And finally, after she turned nineteen, they were married.

Their wedding night, in a drafty hotel room in Scotland, was not a success. The brilliant social critic, scrutinizer of art works, arbiter of cultural taste, looked at his new bride with revulsion. He had rhapsodized about the virtues of "drawing what is really there," but in this case what was really there repelled him. According to both parties, he did not "make her his wife" that night or ever. And six years later, after Effie fell in love with one of his protégés, the marriage was annulled. In his legal deposition Ruskin claimed, about a woman whom several doctors declared perfectly normal and other men found irresistible: "Though her face was beautiful her person was not formed to excite passion. On the contrary there were certain circumstances in her person which completely checked it."

After the calamity of his marriage, Ruskin became enamored of a ten-year-old named Rose La Touche. He was drawn to her blue eyes and milky skin. Reflecting as they did God's perfect purity, the transparent soul; nothing there yet to hide, to lock doors because of, nothing under rough wool blankets at night. He felt cleansed being near her. And when he accidentally saw the shape of her calf as she climbed into a carriage on Norfolk Street outside of her parents' house, she was like an angel, like a fairy, like a doll. She was like the distance between him and the art he observed, so sublime that distance, so full of yearning and thought, that kind of love, from six feet away. And then there was her narrow back, her boyish shoulders, her thinness. He felt safe with her. The straightness of line, her smallness itself protection, and that thought stirred him. A safe place where he could curl up, a pure whiteness against which he could hurl himself. Only in that safe place were dark thoughts allowed to flourish.

And what about Alice? Ruskin wrote of his confusion in her presence on one specific occasion: "It was like being in a dream." And "dream" seemed to be a sort of code word. Ruskin and Dodgson both used it constantly to describe the time they spent with Alice. It was a pretty way of saying beyond the reach of conventional possession: Unreal because I do not want it to be real. Beautiful and impotent in the way dreams are impotent.

After their croquet game, Ruskin drifted off to have a brandy with her father. And Alice was cornered in her mother's boudoir. "Come with me, darlings," Mrs. Liddell had said to her and her sisters. "I am having the most difficult time choosing what to wear to the bishop's dinner." Alice sat on the upholstered stool, with Lorina behind her twisting her hair in the mirror and pursing her lips. Edith was fiddling with the crinoline, as the maid brought out three possible gowns. "Do you think the cream?" her mother asked. "I think the cream."

When Alice was younger she loved to watch her mother dress for a party, to sit in front of the mirror, which was engraved with dripping grapes and leaves. She loved the washbasin with its oriental dragon pattern, her mother's silver brushes, silver capped bottles of perfume, mother-of-pearl jewelry box. The whalebone corset and the crinoline standing in waiting with their complicated set of hooks and ties and fastenings, like pieces of her mother. The shape that she would enter. Alice loved watching the maid drape the pearl necklace over her collarbone, close the buttons of her dress all the way down her back. Her brilliance, taken apart and put together. Swelling larger. Shining hair pinned up. Neck glittering. Fragrance rising. The magnificence of her afterward, bell-shaped and rustling.

But now Alice felt differently. She saw the worn elastic garters with metal clasps on the floor. She stared at the pink line where the corset cut into her mother's ample chest, the crease of freckled bust. Round shoulders. Loose arms. Blotched skin from the bath. She saw her mother repeated and magnified in the oval of the mirror, framed by intricate grapes, spilling pink flesh, pools of softness, surrounding Alice, filling her with disgust.

Edith was standing inside the crinoline and jumping up and down, wearing her mother's black velvet hat with an ostrich feather and her jade necklace. Lorina was bending toward the mirror, begging her mother to let her wear her hair in a low chignon. "Please, Mama, I am old enough." Mrs. Liddell was fastening the garter around a jiggling thigh. Suddenly there was a great pressure to grow up, a push to get on with it, a river of impatience carrying the girls forward, but Alice was not a part of it.

In the past few weeks, the smallest things about her mother had started to repulse her, the smell of her skin, the sound of her chewing, the pale hairs on her arm. The heavy sensual reminders of her mother's existence on earth, the million minor confrontations with her bodily presence that occurred every day. Also repulsive was the tenderness in her own chest, the tiny puffs around her nipples. She was ashamed of the straining cloth at her chest, barely perceptible now. She liked the neatness and flatness of the way she was before. She hated the ballooning and bubbling out of control. She hated the neck growing through the trees in Dodgson's story; the way the body takes away what you have.

⚜

Dodgson and Alice are standing near the wall of the old library, the sky spread out around them, as if they were about to take flight. Alice's hair is falling on her neck, and it is too disorderly for a photograph. What if we just swept it up? Dodgson says, but his hands are trembling and his breath is coming too slowly. He is suddenly overwhelmed with the smell of her skin. He feels the heat of neck beneath fingertips, sees the delicate curve of cheek from behind. His hands are in her hair, but she is almost eleven and he is thirty-one and even though the stories he tells can dip them in water and send them down rabbit holes and turn them upside down, nothing on earth will ever change that.

Moments like these are increasingly common: a flood of emotion, eddies and currents and unmanageable waves, and then a pause, a stop. He is always about to touch her, to feel her; he is always on the edge of Alice, always about to reach her. She is so close, she is sitting on his lap, her weight on his legs, her hair brushing against his face, chestnutty and soft, and her voice is right there, a constant stream of prattle, *Where are my jam tarts? You promised. Are you finished? My legs are falling asleep.*

Is it better the way it is? To feel right next to his face the dusky olive skin, and not to touch; to feel the suspension of all desire, never to be acted upon, diffused; to remain forever in a state of anticipation, the emotion purified and clarified and refined by pain, by the long hours spent observing it and not inhabiting it.

How strange and miraculous and unnerving it is to stumble accidentally on your capacity to open yourself so completely to someone else. To know that you will always feel this way and that time can have no possible effect. To watch it, like a natural wonder, like Niagara Falls, the eternal feeling rising up inside of you, flowing with deafening force, glittering in the sun, even though it is of no practical use.

He returned to his fingertips sweeping her neck. To be stuck forever in that state of almost having. To remain in motion, going toward her and she toward him, though they are never going to reach each other. They are like Zeno's famous paradox: if you divide the space between you and an object in half, and go to that point, and divide the existing space in half and go to that point, you will never actually reach the object. And that is how it is with them. Even when Dodgson and Alice are standing inches apart, the space hangs between them, infinite, lovely, loaded with her scent.

The celebration of the royal wedding crept through Oxford for days. Dodgson could not pass through a single courtyard without seeing workmen hanging paper lanterns and peacock feathers in trees or banging nails for banners and flags. Even at the deanery, Alice and her sisters had planted three small trees in their garden, all of which were named "Edward" after the Prince of Wales. In fact, there were Edwards scattered all over town, Edwards in birdcages and jars, snail Edwards, rock Edwards, and frog Edwards.

The wedding was to take place on March 10, with simultaneous parties planned all over the country, as if the bride and groom could glide down the aisle everywhere at once.

When the morning finally arrived, Alice borrowed one of her mother's cream-colored cards and sent Mr. Dodgson the first invitation she had ever written. *Please accompany me to the celebration this evening. March 10, 1863.* He sent her a written card accepting.

At around six-thirty, gunshots ripped through the university. Dodgson felt them in his chest like the beginning of a war. He and Alice made their way through the cold, past a huge bonfire in Tom Quad. They stood in the crowd, watching the fireworks searing through the sky. Dodgson had gulped down half a glass of champagne at the reception in the common room beforehand and felt stumbly and uplifted. The band struck up a wedding march. Bunches of pearl-colored balloons flew off into the night. Alice slipped her hand in his.

There was the faint smell of burning in the air. He felt the newness of taking her to a public event like this.

"Does everyone have to get married?" Alice asked.

"Not everyone."

"Why don't they?"

"Some people prefer to live alone."

"Mamma says it's wrong not to marry."

"It's certainly unusual."

It amazed him how clearly her feelings showed on her face, beneath the glow and solemnity of the fireworks, how perfectly visible and accessible they were to the most casual observer. He wanted to shield her, cover her up with his jacket, carry her off someplace safer and less public.

Princess Alexandra of Denmark and Prince Edward of Wales were exchanging their vows at that very moment miles away, he told her. The prince was slipping a ring on her finger. He felt the jostle of the crowd, felt the excitement charge through them, as if they were ready to stand with the prince and princess, breathe the words. *With this ring I thee wed.*

"How big is the diamond?" Alice asked.

"About the size of three of your fingernails."

Alice held out her hand to inspect it.

It was like riding on the river with her, experiencing everything twice, the shaking reflection in the river's surface, and then what was happening above. He was watching the events, and he was watching the reflection of the events in Alice. The running river of Alice.

Rice rained down on them from the crowd. Dodgson pulled out his pocket watch and realized that it was half past ten. Bits of rice were stuck in Alice's hair. They watched the balloons fall from the branches. This larger-than-life union, in its own way as outside of reality as Alice and him, the eleven-year-old and the thirty-one-year-old mathematical lecturer by the River Thames.

On the way back to the deanery they passed a set of burning torches suspended on wooden stanchions that spelled out: *May they be happy.* He and Alice stopped in front of it for a moment, her face gold from the flames. He took out a scrap of paper from his inside coat pocket and drew exactly what they saw in front of them, adding burning torches underneath saying, *Certainly not.*

He handed the paper to Alice.

Some days later, Dodgson was leaning over a geometry book at his table with the popular and fashionable William Trevelyan.

"I can't quite see it." Trevelyan smiled, elfin, handsome.

"Have a look at it sideways," Dodgson said, turning the book and pushing it across the table.

Trevelyan stared into the intersecting lines. Dodgson saw the indifference in his face. This young man didn't have to figure out the answer, because the answer was always given to him, and if it wasn't, his bank account would still be filled and the invitations would still be waiting on his mantel.

Dodgson reluctantly wrote out the proof.

I've never been one for maths, Trevelyan said pleasantly.

Dodgson recognized Trevelyan, or rather the boy he could see in his face. Not one of the bullies who beat Dodgson up, stole his books, or turned his things upside down, but one of the prettier boys who stood back and manipulated the others. There was always a Trevelyan.

The Trevelyan at his school had the same narrow face, the same dark blue eyes. He had a thin knife with a pearl handle that he carried in his pocket. His clothes were expensive. He himself was delicate, but he somehow managed to project a kind of sinewy strength. He never fought, never seemed to have anything to do with the violence that burst up around him. He was always slightly bewildered and angelic, off to the side.

A dozen eleven-year-old boys were gathered around him in the clearing in the woods behind the school. Trevelyan said: *If you swallow the toad we shall stop calling you Dodo.* Dodgson's first response was to be flattered that Trevelyan was even talking to him. His tone was friendly, *do this with me*, he seemed to be saying, and Dodgson looked into his dark blue eyes, his handsome, narrow face, and felt himself giving in. There was a milky green pond in front of them, flies breaking the surface.

They were all looking at Dodgson, crowding into him, trying to get a glimpse of the toad. He waved the flies out of his eyes. He looked down at the toad, whose strategy was to stay so still no one would see it, a vein bulging out in its neck. It was a little bigger than a thumbnail and you could see its organs, its blood vessels and veins through its greenish transparent skin. It was not a normal toad. It was a tiny, freakish, see-through toad, and that was why this particular use of it must have suggested itself to Trevelyan: it seemed to call out, in its very distinctive repulsiveness, for an unusual destiny.

Dodgson stood by the side of the pond, wrapped in the green cable scarf his mother had knit for him. The toad took him in with its glossy eyes, its spotted legs clinging to the rock. It seemed to be breathing deeply, as if it knew these might be its last swallows of the March day. And then Dodgson considered the burning feeling he had in his chest when he walked through the mud-colored arches, *A Boy's Guide to Latin* pressed against him. The long meals alone. Some of the boys seemed nice enough when they were by themselves. Like Trevelyan. Like the red-haired bespectacled Patrick who sat next to him, who he happened to know had a book of Wordsworth poems hidden under his mattress, who was now standing somewhat noncommittally in the back of the crowd. They would never mention his stutter again. He heard the warmth in Trevelyan's voice. He thought maybe they could be friends.

So he—who was so fastidious he wrote home when his summer gloves wore out, who was so squeamish he had not long ago called his mother to crush a spider hanging over his bed—reached down for the toad. He took it by its slippery legs, as it waved its arms upside down, and tossed it into his mouth, feeling its tiny feet run down his throat, tickling him as it went down.

He felt like he was going to vomit, like he was going to feel those legs running down his throat for the rest of his life. The juices in his stomach were working on it now, swirling around the toad, alive and frightened in the darkness, clawing the lining of his stomach. Or so he imagined. He looked up, greenish himself now, and expectant.

The sky was brilliantly azure. The sun glared off black rocks. The crowd jeered. He could hear the roughness of the laughter. Trevelyan sat a little ways off on a rock, something cruel and beautiful rising up in him that Dodgson could not help admiring.

After Trevelyan left, Dodgson decided to clear his head with his most recent exercise for Hunt, a scene from *A Midsummer Night's Dream*. Hunt had chosen it. Dodgson would have preferred something with a little more muscle, like *Richard III*. But he had to admit that the exercise was working. His stutter vanished into the thicket of words, the beauty of them. And then he came to the line: *One turf shall serve as pillow for us both. One heart, one bed, two bosoms, and one troth*. He stopped. He put the book down on the mahogany table. He thought of the girls reading it in a few years. Alice's mouth around the words. Alice trying to figure out what they meant. The girl lying in the brambles, her dress bunched up in sleep. The boy lying next to her, his head on a stone, his hand carelessly flung across her waist. Entwined like roses. This was not the kind of education a girl should be receiving.

Think of the sensual rush of the words, the play in the ear. These are the kind of words that could get caught and reverberate, that could lodge in the mind and twist thoughts around themselves like satin blankets. How could this play be given to young girls in good conscience? What if he wrote an even more edited and expurgated version of Shakespeare for Girls? As a child Dodgson had read Bowdler's 1818 version of Shakespeare that occupied an entire shelf of the Croft library, entitled in full:

The Family Shakespeare in Ten Volumes, in which
Nothing Has Been Added to the Original Text, But
Those Words and Phrases are Omitted Which Cannot
With Propriety Be Read in a Family.

And that's what he wanted to write. A Bowdlerized Bowdler. He decided to begin immediately, crossing out the offending lines with violet squiggles and leafing quickly through the play.

~⚜~

"Take me home," Alice said imperiously. She had learned this tone, girlish and theatrical, from someone but from whom?

"Alice, please."

He could hear the pleading in his voice. This was the first time he had seen her without her sisters in two and half weeks. He felt the whole afternoon, the fabric backdrop he had carefully pinned up against the wall, come collapsing down. All because of the jam tarts.

He looked over at Miss Prickett, who was sitting on the divan embroidering a handkerchief.

"She had quite a large breakfast," Miss Prickett said amiably. She could not help him.

"What if I brought the tarts around later?" he asked.

"Later," Alice whined. "That hardly helps me now."

The toy, he thought suddenly, he would bring out the toy.

Several weeks before he had bought the shiny, black mechanical bat at a crowded toy store in London to distract his photographic subjects. He fished it out from a bag beneath his desk.

He held the bat in the palm of his hand and wound the small key in its back. Spreading its silver-dusted wings, it soared across the room with a metallic squeak. Alice reached up to grab it, screaming happily.

When it fell to the ground she insisted on winding it herself. This time it circled above them and flapped its wings right out the window.

They ran to the window and watched as it dove straight toward a tea tray a startled servant was carrying through the courtyard. The servant deftly maneuvered out of its flight path. They looked at each other and started giggling. Alice bent over laughing. The servant looked up. Dodgson bowed politely.

And then he sang for her: *Twinkle, twinkle, little bat, how I wonder what you're at. Up above the world you fly, like a tea-tray in the sky.*

The servant put the tray down on the grass, retrieved the bat from a hedge, and brought it up to the door.

This interlude raised Alice's spirits sufficiently to face the camera. Though she wouldn't look directly at him, wouldn't look at the camera, and instead sat glaring sideways at the wall. Luckily he had been meaning to do some profiles.

"Remember my tarts!" the cruel little thing called over her shoulder as Miss Prickett led her out.

Amazing the things Dodgson would sit through and endure, the wildest accommodations he would make for every whim of Alice's. It did not occur to him that Alice was badly behaved or that he should not have to cater to her so abjectly. But he did feel drained. He lay down on the divan, flapping the bat wings.

So many of the inhabitants of Wonderland were cranky and easily annoyed. Like the duchess who turns to Alice and says, "You don't know much," or the unicorn who calls her a fabulous monster. The strange logic of Wonderland forces Alice to cajole, appease, and flatter a whole series of fantastical beings who are always in a bad mood and always chastising her. Dodgson's creations were so irritable because of how unirritable Dodgson had to be in life. He had invented a world in which every single animal is prickly and sensitive and cranky, all of his annoyance pent up and expressed in animal form.

12

The back of Tudor House on Cheyne Walk was laced with heavy vines which crept across the windows. The day was darker than he would have liked, and the wind blew dried leaves in circles on the dirt. But there were still bushes of yellow roses next to the stairs, and the branches of the weeping cherry tree might make interesting shadows. Dodgson was preparing to photograph Dante Gabriel Rossetti and his family. He had sent his materials by rail, carefully wrapped in paper, and hired a cab from the station. He had taken over a corner of the Rossettis' plum-colored drawing room for a darkroom and studio. He felt the nervousness that other people's houses always inspired in him. And now he was kneeling on the ground pouring the nitrate bath. He had offered to take pictures of the whole family, the artist—poet, his mother, his brother, William, and his sisters, Maria and

Christina. But it was Christina who Dodgson was waiting to meet, Christina, author of *Goblin Market*, who had lured him down from Oxford with all of his trays and bottles.

Dodgson took in the background: stone sky, thin, moody autumn light, chess table, rickety wicker chair, stairway. But it might work with this particular group, the bleak setting.

Just then Rossetti strode out to meet him. Behind him was an older woman in a lace bonnet.

Rossetti had such a compelling face, fuller than Dodgson remembered, that he began to feel glad he had come.

The two men shook hands.

"Mamma, may I introduce you to one of the finest portrait photographers in the country, Reverend William Dodgson," said Rossetti.

"Charles," said Dodgson.

"Apologies," said Rossetti, "I am feeling brotherly toward you already."

Dodgson studied his host. As he leaned against the railing, in his brown checkered pants, his small shiny boots crossed, he looked stocky and strong. His stomach strained against his black waistcoat, but his weight added to his appeal, made him look pleased with himself, like a little Buddha. He had a black beard, a receding hairline, and black eyes with circles under them as dark as bruises. Dodgson framed Rossetti in his camera. You could see his Italian ancestors in his face. The warm-blooded swagger. The intensity. The wine. The bluff. He could see how women would suffer for Rossetti, how they would believe in his ability to reform. The camera caught it before Dodgson did: a helpless sweetness in his lothario's eyes. His crumpled hat.

"I hear that you are now a man of letters," Rossetti said.

Dodgson was pulling out the legs of his tripod.

"N-n-no. Not at all. I—"

Mrs. Rossetti sat perfectly still, gazing into the middle distance, as if she were posing for a painting.

"Nothing to be ashamed of, old man," Rossetti said. "We are all guilty on occasion of that particular sin."

Just then Christina Rossetti floated down the stone steps. Her eyes were huge and pale gray and glittery, with heavy hooded eyelids. She had a high, round forehead, smooth chestnut hair parted in the center, pulled back tightly in a bun, and she wore a wide silk crinoline dress with fashionably flounced pagoda sleeves. Her ethereal presence, Dodgson realized immediately, had nothing to do with the way she looked. She was thinking of something else so visibly, so absorbed in private meditations, that it was hard to focus on her physical aspect; she was not frail or otherworldly and was in fact the slightest bit heavy. As her brother's dramatic features, black hair, black eyes, demanded and sulked for attention, her own pale features seemed to melt into brightness. Dodgson could see how easily Rossetti could eclipse his sister, how his charm would trample over her like an army.

Christina was tall, but the stoop in her shoulders made her look vulnerable.

"My sister Christina," Rossetti said, nodding toward the stairway.

"Delighted," said Dodgson, stepping out from behind his camera.

After a long pause in which he felt she was cataloging all of the things she would rather do before acknowledging his presence, she said vaguely, "How do you do."

Dodgson might have found her manner somewhat irritating had he not thought *Goblin Market* was one of the most brilliant pieces of writing he had ever encountered. Her long poem told the strange story of two sisters tempted at night by goblins selling luscious fruits. *Hug me kiss me suck my juices. Squeezed from goblin fruits for you, Goblin pulp and Goblin dew. Eat me, drink me, love me.*

One of the sisters eats the fruits and gets sick, almost dies. She develops a mysterious addiction to their juices. The other goes out and faces the goblins, who attack, trying to force her to eat their fruits as well. The goblins end up rubbing their juice and pulp all over her. She returns home to let her sister kiss her and suck her in order to consume the forbidden juices and save her life. The poem was so unlike the insipid jingles normally read to children that many people had trouble understanding it. But to Dodgson it was as familiar as if he had written it himself. A children's story about sisters and goblins. An adult story about the sensual tussle. Appetite suppressed and unsuppressed. Love between siblings that curved and ripened and soured like certain fruits. He had stayed up all night after reading it, pacing through his room, jealous and inspired and enraged and disturbed. The poem was wild and uncontrolled, like a dream. A story without structure or logic, angry-colored fragments that flew at you from all directions.

Dodgson looked through the viewfinder at the Rossettis scattered across the garden like they had been blown by the wind. Most of the time he had to pose families, tell them not to bunch together and stare at the camera so predictably. But the Rossettis seemed to focus off in different directions; they seemed to drift naturally to opposite edges of the frame.

He was eager to photograph Christina. Such a strange combination of elegance and awkwardness she was, an astonishingly beautiful woman who seemed to have nothing but indifference bordering on mild distaste for her own beauty. He watched her fiddle with the brooch at her neck. There was something childlike and mischievous about her, which may have been the goblin's chant running through his mind: *Citrons and dates, Grapes for the asking, Pears red with basking, Out in the sun, Plums on their twigs, Pluck them and suck them, Pomegranates, figs.* The tune you hear at night; that other tune.

He pulled out the chair next to the chess table for Mrs. Rossetti and asked Christina if she minded sitting on the stairs.

She agreed, but then she wouldn't look at the camera. Each time he thought he had her, her huge, hooded eyes slipped away at the last moment. She had been Jesus and the Virgin Mary and countless other things for her brother. She must have spent hours in the paint fumes of the studio, sitting for each painting. But she would not look for forty-five seconds at his camera.

The two sisters in her poem fold into one: the one who eats, and the one who does not. They cling to each other like sailors in a shipwreck.

The pale sun shone through the low-hanging branches of the cherry.

"Christina, he can't get the likeness if you keep turning," Rossetti said.

She looked at Dodgson helplessly.

The words of the poem looped through his mind: *Though goblins coaxed and caught her, Bullied and besought her,*

Scratched her, pinched her black as ink, Kicked and knocked her, Mauled and Mocked her, Lizzie uttered not a word.

How strange that she would put a dream—it must have been a dream—right out there, pinned open, for everyone to see.

All his photographs of her would be profiles, glowing half-moons.

"I'm afraid I can't," she said to Dodgson afterward. "I'm terribly sorry. It's not you. I can't face most of the world properly."

He recognized the trait.

"I-I-I wonder if you m-m-might be interested in l-looking at my children's story when I've finished it?"

Rossetti banged the door as he went inside.

"Certainly," said Christina. "I would be honored."

As Dodgson packed up his equipment, Rossetti and a friend, Arthur Munby, who had just arrived, were sitting by the window in the drawing room, drinking whiskey and water. Munby was a strikingly handsome man, with glossy black hair and a large beard. He was a civil servant, poet, and a man about town. He also secretly married a charwoman.

The lace curtains were pulled back. Rossetti's underwater women were staring out from the walls.

Dodgson sat on the floor rolling each bottle, tray, and funnel in paper and placing them in a box.

"Brilliant piece in *Fraser's*, by the way," Rossetti said.

Munby smiled shyly.

"Another," Rossetti said, holding up his glass to the maid, a plain girl with thick arms.

"Lucy is looking well," said Munby when she left the room.

"I suppose," Rossetti said. "Are you still going on about the rights of the working woman?"

"I am."

"Myself, I have enough trouble with the women of our own class."

"True."

"All talk though, aren't you?"

"I suppose." Munby shrugged.

"Dodgson," Rossetti said, "Munby has quite an impressive collection of photographs of working women, charwomen, and scullery maids, dirty and bare-armed and all that. He finds them on the street and arranges to have their likeness taken."

Munby flushed.

"I should love to see them," Dodgson said politely, carefully packing his lens. But in fact, the idea of this bizarre collection wrapped in tissue in the back of a dark armoire unsettled him.

"*Chaqu'un à son goût*, I suppose," Rossetti said.

Dodgson spent the next day making prints. He labeled each of the Rossettis and spread them out on his desk. There was something to be said for the sepia that washed through photographs, the distinctive brown, with the faintest trace of green, that faded into rich cream. This was a color that soothed and softened, slowed down and made melancholy the world around it. A perpetual, stylized dusk. Most remarkable was what sepia did to Christina's eyes. The color showed them more clearly than one could see in normal light, her expression refined and projected and magnified and somehow sorted out and made sense of. Sepia was the perfect medium for eyes.

He packed up the Rossettis, wrapping them in paper to be sent along to Cheyne Walk, then returned to his darkroom to do Alices. He was particularly fond of the negative of Alice as a Chinaman, in a red satin tunic embroidered with dragons with a triangular straw hat balanced on her head. Her pointy un-soft little face looked so ageless. Other children had more fat on their faces—that is what it was—a softness that makes them seem hazy and undefined, that gives you a visual cue: they are yet to become. Alice never had that. She already was.

As he pressed the plate against the coated paper, he caught Alice's gaze through the glass and felt a guilty rush of pleasure. Here was Alice reproduced, an infinite number of tiny Alices for his private viewing, alone with him in the semidarkness. He shook the prints and hung them. One, two, three. The repetitiveness of the work soothed him.

Alice loved the darkroom. She loved standing next to him over the basins, watching the images slowly appear on the glass plates. Wait for me outside, he would tell her, but she would stand folded in the curtains. Alice had a way of obeying the letter of a command and ignoring its spirit. Right now Alice wasn't standing in the curtains. He happened to know from Miss Prickett, she was out picking flowers for her mother's musical evening for the crown Prince of Denmark, to which he had not been invited, and about which he was trying hard not to feel snubbed.

Alice. Alice and another Alice. In front of flame-colored roses. Great conjurer, master creator, lonely landscapist, Dodgson was making more Alices and might never stop. He knew that her parents no longer wanted his photographs, and Alice herself already had copies of them all pressed between the leaves of her keepsake book. Only he seemed to have an insatiable curiosity, an insatiable, almost scientific need to experiment with his technique. What if I soak it for just a second more? What if it's just a shade lighter? Only he seemed to have the desire to see Alice in every gradation of light. At this point, Dodgson knew that more photographs would be superfluous, wasteful, no longer art, because there were too many of them. They were clichés, like so many painted sunsets lying in attics across the countryside. And yet he was never satisfied, feeling the warm egg white mixture wash over his hands and the slippery print of Alice in red satin emerging from its redolent dip.

Suddenly he was touching her face, he was rubbing her features out with his finger. He held it up. It was quite alarming, her familiar hair hanging over an unfamiliar face, its features distorted. He reached for the rest of the prints and ruined them all, smearing and smudging every single one. They were waiting innocently in the tray, floating like children in a bath. A glass measure of acid splashed on his arm. First came cold and then burning. He quickly poured a pitcher of water on it, but the burning was still there, and when he stepped out of the darkroom, his arm was dark red and throbbing with pain. He wondered if it would scar.

13

The migraine started behind his left eye, a sharp spiraling pain that rocked through the inside of his skull. He felt nausea rising through him. And then he saw bright flashes in front of his eyes, yellow stripes of light with green outlines that hung in the air and then vanished. He could feel the pressure against bone. His brain craving darkness. When it finally subsided, he got up and went to his desk. He had been putting it off for months, and Alice had been asking and asking.

The blank piece of paper lay in front of him. The story seemed out of his reach—not that he couldn't remember it, but he couldn't get to it. Like the shore on the foggy boat ride. He could barely make out its outlines through the silver thickness. He thought of Alice lying on the ground, her hands behind her head, her face sticky from the heat. Her socks and shoes a little ways off by the river. He picked up his pen and began. *Alice*

was beginning to get very tired of sitting by her sister on the
bank, and of having nothing to do.

The day faded. The sky was the color of ink. And still he sat
at his desk, writing, his body flooded with a deep sense of calm,
as if the headache that had clenched his muscles left them
soothed and massaged.

He scribbled pictures of Alice in the margins as he went
along. But his two-dimensional Alice, with her bedraggled dark
hair and puffy sleeves, wasn't right. He tore up page after page.
There was a trapped-looking apprehension in her enormous
eyes that he did not intend. He began again, the square neck of
the dress, the Cupid's bow mouth, the hair, longer, curling, and
then, her eyes, black and expressive, but again, she was scared.
He held up the sketch so he could see it. But it was crude: lines
groping for a face, like hands reaching out in the dark.

He turned the drawing around and around and tried to
think his way through. He had been trying for a kind of festive
surprise. But in the story she was growing and shrinking at an
alarming rate. Her neck had grown into the trees. *She tried to*
bring her head down to her hands and was delighted to find
that her neck would bend about easily in every direction, like
a serpent. Maybe fear was not so far off.

He looked down at the manuscript. Page sixty-three. His
room was dark except for the circle of lamplight that fell over
the pages on his desk. He felt as if he were on a luminous island, in the dark floating sea of his library. Navigating his way
to the fireplace, he poured himself a glass of sherry from the
decanter on the mantel and then sat down to finish. He finally
fell asleep at the desk, the lamp still burning, his head pillowed
by the first chapters of *Alice's Adventures under Ground.*

Dodgson dreamed that Alice was lying in a canopy bed. A kitten was chanting softly, then louder and louder: *Off with her head! Off with her head!* It began hissing and spitting and showing its teeth. *Off with her head! Off with her head!* The crescendoing rhythm became unbearable. He rushed into the room and in one motion twisted off Alice's head, which, to his surprise, came off like a cork. Then he realized what he had done. Blood flowed from her neck, soaking the sheets, the quilts, the rug. He held her nightgowned body, cradling it, covered in blood himself. As the bed rocked, the blood became a pool, and they floated on it like a boat. He woke up suddenly, his heart beating like it was trying to fly out of his chest, the sheets wet with sweat. He sat on the side of the bed without moving. He looked up at the pale gray sky. And then he put on a robe, went over to his desk, and began charting out his effort to replace the 12th Axiom of Euclid, his thoughts escaping to the letters in front of him. Gathering themselves. Focusing on the numbers.

In the introduction to a mathematical tract, *Curiosa Mathematica, Part II, Pillow Problems, Thought Out During Sleepless Nights*, Dodgson once wrote about mathematics as escape. He explained that "There are mental troubles much worse than mere worry, for which an absorbing object of thought may serve as a remedy. . . . There are blasphemous thoughts, which dart unbidden into the most reverent souls; there are unholy thoughts, which torture, with their hateful presence, the fancy that would fain be pure."

Dodgson knew that there were stronger remedies for these hateful fantasies than mathematics. He had once been offered opium by a man named Finn, who lived across the hall from him in Christ Church. With blondish hair plastered to his forehead, hooded eyelids that never seemed entirely open, and a short, stubbly beard, Dodgson always thought Finn looked like a sea otter emerging from a nap. A group of students had experimented with the drug in his room. Pillows on the floor. Staying up until dawn. Sleeping through the next day. The great literary cult of being out of your senses. Dodgson was attracted to the idea of being drugged, rising out of himself, escaping the confines of his own experience, losing himself, even temporarily. He remembered how Finn described it. They are wrong about opium, Finn had said. It doesn't give you dreams. It takes them away.

At around the same time, Dodgson's friend Southey had brought him some laudanum for his headaches from the druggist on High Street. The big brown bottle had a handmade hexagonal label, the ink slightly runny: tincture of opium. But Dodgson could never quite bring himself to try it, no matter how bad his headaches got. He was afraid of who he might become.

So he himself had never tasted opium. But one of the odder fabrications of his children's story was an opium-sucking insect who sits in a cloud of smoke, feeling nothing. *A large blue caterpillar, which was sitting with its arms folded, quietly smoking a long hookah, and taking not the smallest notice of her or of anything else.* Which was something Dodgson sometimes wished. That she would enter a room and he would barely notice.

⚜

Alice was posing in front of the fireplace, her head tilted upward with her hands behind her back. Dodgson was drawing a portrait.

Edith stood a few feet away in a white muslin dress, trying to project her wish outward, like a round white fruit waiting to be picked.

"I'm tired," Alice said.

"Words are arbitrary, you know," Dodgson said, not lifting his eyes from the paper. "One could say x instead of tired. Alice is x by the fireplace."

"I am still tired." Alice sulked. She put one hand against the brick. Her blue dress had a wide ruffle sleeve.

"Look." He showed her the half-drawn sketch with flowing curly hair.

"That is not my hair."

The heavy red drapes were almost closed over the tall panes; a thin stripe of light fell across the floor. Edith felt the rejection alive in the room.

The renowned art critic John Ruskin now gave Alice drawing lessons. Edith knew how renowned he was because her parents made so much of his coming. "It is a privilege that he wants to teach you, darling," her mother told Alice when she complained that she didn't want to learn drawing. The other day he was having tea alone in the sitting room with Alice, guiding her hand through a sketch of the cathedral, when the Liddells came home unexpectedly from a luncheon party. Ruskin told Alice, who told Edith, this: when her parents walked in the door it felt like the stars were suddenly blown out by the wind.

Edith had never understood why Alice should be so much preferred. Edith was good, but Alice's badness always seemed to be more fascinating to everyone around them, even though they said they deplored it. Before Mr. Dodgson arrived, for instance, Alice ran through the parlor in her nightgown shouting, "I *am* Heathcliff! I *am* Heathcliff."

"Alice, stop that immediately," said Mrs. Liddell, but Edith could hear the admiration in her voice. *Wuthering Heights* was a favorite of her mother's. She once gathered them into bed with her and told them the plot.

But that was the maddening thing—that rules did not apply to Alice, or that they bent and shifted before her mildest whims. Every detail in the family arrangements seemed to cry out Alice's singularity: they even had to eat eggs three times a week because that was the only breakfast Alice would think of taking a few bites of.

The only sound in the room was the scratching of pen on paper.

"I'm going to move," Alice said without moving.

Dodgson stopped and tucked the drawing pad under his arm.

"We shall finish another time then."

Alice darted across the room, leaving Edith standing there in her white dress. There was a glow between Alice and Mr. Dodgson and it hurt to be outside of that glow.

As she watched Alice disappear up the stairs, Edith remembered how they used to fight, how they would pull each other's hair until their scalps were red, how terrifying it was; she remembered their relief when their nurse would enter the room, because they knew that this kind of fighting was not just childish, it was animal rage, infinite and unloosed; on their arms were little arcs of crimson from fingernails, and she knew in her heart that if they were left alone they would rip each other apart.

The rawness was still there. Though they played together on the piano, just the night before, each note loud, wishful, blocking the other out.

Why shouldn't it be *Edith's Adventures under Ground?*

Dodgson wrapped his charcoal in tissue, put it in his pocket, and picked up his sketchbook.

Edith took his hand and showed him to the door.

She knew that Mr. Dodgson did not find her interesting. He did not think she was worth drawing. But that knowledge had not stopped her from putting on one of her best dresses that morning or running downstairs to greet him at the door. By now she knew she would be unhappy every time she tried to impress him, mostly because she would fail. She would feel frantically alone, like there was something monstrously wrong with her, like she would be a Miss Liddell for the rest of her life, like her aunts Amelia and Charlotte, getting wrinkled and fat, with nothing but puddings and romances and the Bible to comfort her. Maybe she would become religious, because the Good Lord was the only one who would have her, as she once heard her mother say about Aunt Amelia. If she could just leave Dodgson alone, she might feel better. She couldn't though. She got too much pleasure out of the situation. Like pulling the skin off her cuticles until they bled.

The night before, Lorina and Alice were playing Ballroom in Ina's room and they had locked Edith out. She sat on the floor in the hallway, her knees curled under her nightgown. She could hear them giggle and knock into walls as they glided through the room in each other's arms. She hated the feeling of being locked out, but she was used to it. She was locked out of everything. Can I go riding with Papa? she asked her mother. You are not nearly old enough, her mother said. But somehow when she was old enough there would be no ponies, or Papa wouldn't have time, and this was how it always was.

Her situation reminded her of the story her father used to tell her about Hades and the underworld: she felt like a special punishment had been devised, where the whole world was dangled in front of her by her older sisters, but whenever she reached for it, it was gone.

❦

"Why on earth wouldn't you publish it?" asked Macdonald.

He was walking quickly next to Dodgson. The light was strange. The sky was dark gray, but the buildings glowed bright pink. They were on their way back from High Street.

"Hard to explain," Dodgson said.

Originally he viewed the Alice story as a private correspondence. But the more people he showed it to, the more comfortable he felt. He was relieved when they responded with amusement. And so the idea of publication was starting to draw him in. Like light under a closed door.

"What do you think of the title?" Dodgson asked. He couldn't stop changing words around, picking at the manuscript like a scab.

"Perfectly adequate unless you have another in mind."

Dodgson was thinking of changing Alice's story from *Alice's Adventures under Ground* to *Alice's Adventures in Wonderland*. Under ground had darker connotations, making one think of coffins and criminals. He preferred Wonderland, which brought to the fore the more-lighthearted aspects of the place.

"It seems so public."

"Yes, some might say that's the point."

"Well, of course."

"I must say I cannot understand your hesitation," Macdonald said. "Not with a story like this."

Macdonald himself was working on a children's book called *The Light Princess*, about a princess without gravity who floated into the air. *The day was so sultry that the little girl was wrapped in nothing less ethereal than slumber itself.* Eventually she meets a prince and learns to fall. Macdonald had just received a letter from John Ruskin objecting that the manuscript was too amorous and further insisting that the scenes of the prince and princess swimming in the moonlight could do serious harm to young readers.

The two men continued their walk in silence. The sky darkened. But the buildings were still pink, the late-afternoon light collecting in the windows, in pink gold squares.

"Perhaps it's a bit undignified," Dodgson said finally.

The idea of attaching his name to his story felt dangerous. Like a man tied to a rock by the ocean in the middle of a storm.

"Dignity?" Macdonald raised his eyebrows.

In the distance they heard thunder. They rounded the corner of the cathedral and saw Mrs. Liddell walking toward them carrying her new baby, with Miss Prickett pushing the perambulator.

From all of the doubt, Dodgson shook out the knowledge that his story was good.

What about Macdonald's *Light Princess?* He found it charming and light as the title suggested, but there was something else. A hollowness in the princess's laughter. She can laugh but she cannot feel. Even when her father whips her. Even when the prince is slowly drowning in the lake and almost dies. Because she has no gravity, has known no sadness. She was somewhat frightening to Dodgson. Her hysterical empty laughter. Floating to the ceiling. Until she falls in love.

Mrs. Liddell was holding the baby as if she were too heavy. Under her white lace bonnet, the baby's face was pink, her nose turned up. Almost like a pig, Dodgson caught himself thinking.

They took off their hats.

"Gentlemen," she said, walking past.

"How about a nom de plume then?" said Macdonald.

Dodgson thought. The wildest part of him circulated. His stories read to children in their beds, his characters there in the steady breathing of sleeping girls.

Dodgson searched for a name that suited the spirit of the venture.

"What would you think of Charles Dares?"

"Too newspaperish," said Macdonald. "Charles Dares Exposes Corruption in the House of Lords."

They reached Dodgson's rooms.

"I brought you a few likenesses of the girls," Dodgson said. "I had almost forgotten."

He handed Macdonald the photographs of his daughters, two of Irene and one of Lily. He had taken the photographs at their house in Hampstead three weeks earlier.

Back in his rooms, Dodgson sat with a glass of sherry, mulling over the name in his head. He wanted to create a pseudonym by alchemy, by breaking down the elements of his real name and turning it into something else. Charles Lutwidge Dodgson. The first one he came up with was Edgar Cuthwellis.

❧

Thick books were piled on the table in front of him, on his lap, and on the floor next to his feet. He had taken a small carrel next to the high sunny window. He had no students coming by, and on such a beautiful afternoon the library was empty. Dodgson had decided to approach the problem of his nightmares scientifically. His dreams had gotten progressively worse. He knew he had no more claim to them than he would to strangers who brushed up against him on a city street. But still they made him anxious. He had stopped remembering them whole, but they left traces that took hours to disappear. The sound of tearing cloth. The gold flash of shoulder blades. Something darkening the edges of thought.

Who are you? asks the caterpillar in the story he was writing. Alice replies, *I hardly know, sir, just at present—at least I know who I was when I woke up this morning, but I think I must have been changed several times since then.* All kinds of creatures are constantly asking Alice who she is and she is constantly demurring. And that was how Dodgson felt as he sat in the library: the constant nagging question, the absence of answer.

After skimming through several books, D. Watson Bradshaw's *The Anatomy of Dyspepsia* among them, he found that bad digestion is one of the primary causes of nightmares. A badly cooked rack of lamb can lead to murderous dreams, and an excess of shellfish can unloose all sorts of nervousness.

Dodgson's back was stiff from sitting and he stretched his

arms over his head. Out the window was a group of under-graduates racing through the courtyard on tilted armchairs, propelling themselves toward one another across the grass. This practice was called "tilting," and there was a tilting mania that spring. As far as he could tell, the point of these elaborate tournaments seemed to be to crash violently in the middle. Dodgson looked away. He always found it unnerving to watch. He didn't like the visual image of unbalance, of imminent falls.

June 4, 1863

Three cups water
1/2 pear
1/4 slice toast
one cup tea

The fast is starting to achieve its purpose—to sim-plify the craving—to shed the layer of fat—the curves of stomach and hips—the pocket of flesh around my waist.

My stomach churns & works on nonexistent food—It feels as if there are knots tying and untying them-selves—If only one could rid oneself of flesh entirely—break down the cells and elements—crack open the infirm body & become something else entirely.

I attempt to concentrate on Alice's story—Perversely my thoughts turn to food, but with disgust—dripping butter on bread, yellow, greasy—cakes filled with sugary creams that are horrible in their heavi-ness—roast beef sitting in bloody juices—every morsel of food I contemplate putting in my mouth suddenly viewed under a microscope—reduced to its elements, all things are repellent. And then of course the pages themselves swell with hunger—eat me, drink me— Alice's potion tasting of roast beef, cherry tart, custard, pineapple, roast turkey, toffy, and hot buttered toast.

I fall asleep with my stomach curling over from hunger. The pain is clarifying. I dream of an Alice-shaped biscuit, and eat it headfirst.

14

Hunt came to the door barefoot in his robe. He had been sleeping when he heard the servant's tentative knock. It was half past seven. The air was still cool and silky.

Standing framed by the doorway was Dodgson.

He had never had a visitor at this hour.

Dodgson was twisting his hat in his hands. He looked more agitated than Hunt had ever seen him. The bones at his temple were too prominent. His collar was loose. He had lost weight since Hunt had seen him two weeks before. He did not look well.

"Would you like to come in?"

Dodgson shook his head.

"Is everything all right?"

Hunt saw that Dodgson was trying to speak, his lips pursed, his throat straining around phantom words.

He thrust a leather folder into Hunt's hands.

"What is this?" said Hunt.

Dodgson looked at him helplessly.

A dog barked on the lawn.

"Breathe," said Hunt.

Dodgson took several deep breaths and then spoke. "I b-b-brought some photographs."

Hunt had no idea what to make of this.

"Good-bye," said Dodgson, and he turned and walked through the gate.

After Dodgson left, Hunt sat down at his desk. He untied the leather folder and took out the photographs. It was Dean Liddell's daughter, wasn't it? What was her name, Lorina, Alice? There was one of her asleep on top of a fur throw. There was one of her turned sideways facing a wall. Portraits of a little girl. He leafed through all of the photographs. But that was all there was.

His mind worked on the photographs, impressive examples of the form, but what did they mean? Why was Dodgson so shaken? The faces were serious and beautiful. They were like words, perfectly formed, luminous words, but he couldn't quite read them.

Outside, the dogs chased each other in circles. One bit at the flank of the other. A low rumble of growls. He was supposed to spend the morning editing an article on bone classification for the *Anthropological Review*. Cranium shapes. Thorough but uninspired. And now here were these photographs. Nos. 1,008–17.

He could see the affection in the photographs. He could see the time and the care and reverence that went into them. Clearly, the child meant something to him. He was sharing her with Hunt the way one shares a secret. But why? Perhaps this was simply an enactment of the stutter on a new stage. Another fumbled utterance. Hunt was reminded of the limitations of his occupation, and possibly himself.

He turned back to the article's third paragraph about forehead height.

> *June 13, 1863*
>
> *I walked to Portsdown Road & the city felt thick and clotted in my lungs—the black door looked permanent & forbidding—an ancient pagan edifice like Stonehenge.*
>
> *And then there was the fatigue—the overwhelming exhaustion—is there no other way to explain it?—that takes over when I am required to meet someone with whom I am barely acquainted. The thought of drinking a cup of tea with John Tenniel was so daunting that I was completely drained in advance.*
>
> *Have I adequately conveyed the inauspicious beginning?*
>
> *Tenniel is a tall, red-haired man with voluminous whiskers, confident & solid. He lost one eye in a fencing accident with his father, which gives him the unusual habit of turning his chiseled face slightly to a profile as he speaks—He carries himself more like an officer in the army than a children's book illustrator, I must say—and his presence has a strange effect, making me more myself, a parody of myself: I fluttered around like a butterfly, dropping my coat & stuttering out a hello like an apology.*

He led me into his forest-green, bookless study, with a silver head of armor mounted on the mantel and a slightly tarnished sword above the fireplace. I looked anxiously at the framed Tenniels on the wall as if they were signposts: a street urchin out of Dickens, two women in Arabian veils reclining on a divan, and a dark-haired woman borne into the sky by an angel.

Only then did I remember hearing that Tenniel's wife Julia had died of consumption soon after they married.

Please sit down, he said.

A cup of tea, a word about low-lying clouds, the usual things.

On his oak desk was an unfinished drawing for Punch, *several colored bottles of ink, ivory pens, a loud clock under a glass dome, and three newspapers. No sign of Alice.*

Let us go directly to business, then, shall we? he said.

Business. The word trampled through me. He might have said commerce. Marketplace. Money. They all seem equally incongruous and jarring.

He took his portfolio out of a drawer and slid it across the desk. My hands were almost shaking as I opened it. Why did I ever agree to publication? Why did I agree to let someone else interpret my story? Why have I laid myself bare before this man I hardly know? My fingers fumbled with the portfolio strings.

And then came a great confusion—I experienced it in the opening—like unwrapping a gift—the mind for a

moment confronted with what it wants. For the first
time I was aware of seeking out a twin—someone who
swims down to the depths & sees the pitch-black ter-
rain—who can feel it out with me. A strange image, I
must admit—envisioned suddenly as a Tenniel sketch—
black brush strokes, heavy hair & eyebrows—Tenniel &
I strolling hand in hand in a place before words. If we
could somehow come across the story together—shin-
ing in the glory of its original intentions—not as it is
but as it should be—splotches & smudges & shapes of
bright color—in the midst of forming themselves—
    I can smell the leather as I open it & lift the layer
of paper from the drawings. Has he understood me?
With a bewildering combination of relief & disappoint-
ment, I see that he has not—His Alice is not my Alice—
She is blond, vapid, lovely, of the type that people are so
fond of thse days. He has made the story sweet &
whimsical, and erased almost all traces of darkness—
there is something in the eyes though, eyelashes too
thick and heavy, forehead too high. The drawings are
skilled—more skilled than my own crude sketches, cer-
tainly—his Wonderland is less wild & menacing, his
Alice washed out & pretty & not at all like my black-
eyed, sparkling, intense little creature. He will never see
Alice. He has transformed my dreams into a pastel fan-
tasy populated by harmless creatures & blond girls.
Perfect.

After leaving Tenniel's, Dodgson hurled his baggage onto
the rack and settled into his black leather seat. He pulled open

the curtain so that he could look out at the station. He watched people hurry across the platform, with porters behind them, carrying large suitcases on their heads. He had forgotten to buy the paper. Across the platform, the 5:15 to Hastings began to slide out of the station. He thought of Tenniel's drawings printed in his book. *Alice's Adventures under Ground.* The story irrevocably slipped out of his hands. An older woman in a plaid dress, carrying a large hatbox, stumbled unsteadily into the seat across from him. Behind her was a tall, blond girl he assumed was her daughter. Neither of them looked directly at him, which Dodgson appreciated.

The sudden movement of the train startled him. He could see the dirtiest parts of London slip past him. Smokestacks shooting swirls of soot. Petticoats flapping on clotheslines strung out between the windows of a building. The ripple of a curtain, the sudden curiosity about the people who lived behind it. The strange flash of intimacy and transplantation. The blond girl pulled a book from her bag. The train rocked and swayed, unloosing bits of the past.

The summer he was eighteen his father gave him a formal introduction to the opposite sex. He had grown four inches that year and felt, in his own body, like a houseguest overstaying his welcome. The new doctor, who lived half a mile away from the large three-story Georgian rectory, had two daughters around his age. He had heard about them extensively in letters from his sisters. And his father had invited them for tea while his mother and sisters were away visiting his aunt.

He remembered the girls sweeping into the rectory with their father, their apple-green dresses, pink cashmere shawls, heart-shaped faces, rumpled blond ringlets, blue eyes like almonds. He saw their arrival reflected on his father's face, the admiration.

The archdeacon liked women. And they reciprocated. Dodgson heard a thickness in his father's voice when he talked to women, something caught in his throat. He could hear it now, *I've heard you play beautifully*. Their large blue eyes tilted up to him. *Oh, no, we are barely able to pound out a few notes*. These exchanges always bothered Dodgson. He could feel his father inviting him to speak to the girls. To throw his presence through the room, like heat from a fire.

"Sugar?"

"Yes, please."

They listened to the sound of tea pouring into cups.

The taller one's hands were constantly in her hair, pulling and stroking it. She shot a glance at her sister, who burst into giggles. Everything was funny to these sisters, as if the mere fact of romantic availability endowed the most banal events with comic brilliance.

Their fathers talked about the latest humiliation of the local MP, but the girls seemed to have an understanding that ran like a bright strand of ribbon between them. They seemed to be having some other conversation beneath the surface that had no obvious connection to anything around them.

He could hear his father's voice. *It is entirely possible he thought he could get away with it. The cabinet is behind him*. His voice was the rich background, like a medieval tapestry, tangled leaves and black pools, behind a unicorn.

How was the afternoon supposed to end? An intrigue? An understanding? A frisson? Perhaps simply a preference.

When the tall one leaned over to pour more milk into her

tea, he noticed the small buttons running all the way down the back of her dress. Seeing them reminded him of the day his father took him to the Royal Academy, the feeling he had in front of Turner's "Peace—Burial at Sea." The feeling of standing in front of a painting whose reputation has been expounded to you, whose image has engraved itself in your mind long before you lay eyes on it, whose glory and beauty has been extolled, and then finally seeing it and feeling nothing. Standing there in the drafty museum and realizing that it has left you cold.

The girls left, trailing ribbons. His father vanished into his study. The Turner dissolved into smoke-colored wisps, gray and ordinary like a bleak autumn day, nothing transporting about it. His father had stood expectant and filled with the painting. Dodgson didn't understand then, one has one's own Turners locked away, one's private inspirations, that are uniquely framed and painted to one's particular tastes. Still, he sometimes found it hard not to share in the warm collusion, the spirited feeling about the beauty of a particular set of brush strokes. To be there, with his father, behind the closed door of the study.

Dodgson got up, squeezed past the ticket taker, down the corridor, and stood at the intersection between cars. Strands of smoke blew past. He could feel the wind rushing through his hair, could taste it in his mouth.

The blond sisters and Joseph Turner had not been the only passions he couldn't share with his father. The truth, which he had hidden for all of these years, was that he stopped feeling certain about God. If he believed in God, it was not at all in the way he was supposed to. God was like a childhood home that your father has sold out from under you; a place you live in your dreams, that you haven't seen in years. When he was at Oxford, deciding whether to accept a religious vocation, with all of the dons telling him how suited he was to the calling, with all of the outside signs pointing in that direction, with no betrothal in sight, even in the deepest layers of fantasy, he felt nothing. Behind all of the mathematics, all of the theorems, he could not be sure of a benign presence. Why if not whimsical or cruel would God create a stooped paradox like himself; a sense of morality shattered by temptation; an archdeacon's son, an arch sinner?

In 1860, during the great debate over evolution in the new university museum, Dodgson had felt himself going over to the side of the apes. "And in what way, sir, are you suggesting that you are descended from the apes, through your grandmother or grandfather?" demanded the bishop, Soapy Sam Wilberforce, of Thomas Huxley, the skinny young scientist chosen to represent Darwin. Laughter rocked through the audience. The religious students and dons were relieved to hear Their Side take the point. But in truth it was easier for him to feel the apes running through his blood than the angels. He felt the animal, the gross bodily greed, the mute desire, coiled inside him. An elderly woman fainted from the excitement during the final arguments and was carried out by two students. Dodgson felt light-headed too, as if the last traces of his skepticism were being carried out along with her. Though he would never admit it to anyone, his father least of all. He thought it. Darwin might be right.

Neither Dodgson's faith nor his skepticism was as enduring as he sometimes felt them to be. He lived with each of them, partially, unsatisfactorily, but passionately. Like the sun pouring through patches of clouds and *The Origin of Species* chapters 4–7 ("Natural Selection" through "Instinct"), and the Bible minus miracles. His belief in both was intermittent, selective. Though they might seem contradictory and impossible, both ideas existed for him, the familiar burnished leather-bound God of his childhood and the exciting Darwin of his mid-twenties; like a wife and mistress for another kind of man.

With such confusion, he could hardly take full religious orders, as his father pressured him to do. So he became a mathematical lecturer. Which, it seemed to him, mostly involved sitting at his desk feeling leaden and unbrilliant. He waited for inspiration in the numbers that unfolded diligently down the page. Instead, he plodded. Momentary bursts of ambition notwithstanding, he knew he was a mediocre mathematician. He had always worked hard, been adequate. But he was never going to join Euclid, Pascal. He was not going to contribute, seriously contribute, that is, to the field. He would doodle in the margins of logic. He would teach three or four wayward boys how to solve a proof. If he was lucky.

He used to see a brilliant academic career as a way back into his father's good graces, but it didn't work. Not entirely. He knew his father was disappointed in him. The archdeacon had imagined an old age surrounded by grandchildren, imagined his oldest son, the heir to his gift for mathematics, reproducing numerically, not just producing numbers. He told him about the grandchildren of his neighbors with a kind of over-enthusiasm that contained within it, like a letter discreetly placed in an envelope, a reproach. He wanted grandchildren, little Charles, a repeat of his son but without the stutter. The startling barrenness of his children seemed a strange trick nature was playing on him after his own biological largesse. Eleven children. Certain posterity. Immortality. His virtues and talents, embedded in a new set of Dodgsons. It seemed that, at least, Dodgson could have given him instead of an interminable fairy tale, three mathematical tracts, and countless puzzles: himself perhaps the greatest one.

Dodgson walked back to his seat through the rattling car. He pressed his forehead against the window. Hedges and brick houses blurred past, vast green spaces reduced into a fraction of a second. Space compressed in time. Whole lives condensed and left behind. The woman across from him in the feather hat had fallen asleep under a wool lap throw, her lips partly open. The daughter's face was blocked by her book.

What if he looked out the window of the moving train and nothing changed? A small brick house with a cow tied to a tree always there out the window. Nothing passing, nothing pulled backward, everything there, no matter how fast the train moved, everything fixed. One frame in the window as you move.

He was eight. His sister Elizabeth was ten. He opened the door to her room late one afternoon, twisting and rattling the knob till it gave, in order to retrieve the puppet theater he had left there after that morning's rehearsal, and she was standing there naked. Dressing for the guests. He instantly realized that he should have known. He slammed the door. Which had never been more than three quarters open. He had seen an expanse of peach-pink skin rising up and spreading through the room. And then he focused again, his sister's neck, shoulder blades, back, buttocks, thighs.

A few minutes later, his ordinary sister in an aubergine dress, damp hair combed neatly into a bun, padded down the stairs to meet the guests. Her round brown eyes met his, emptied of any unusual occurrence. That emptiness hung between them, like humidity, like thick summer air, this chance event, this thing that could not possibly have been his fault. But then, the guilt made him nauseous, made it impossible for him to eat the candied apricots the nurse brought up to the nursery later that evening. The brand new idea, which was not simply an idea of his sister without clothes. Though only seconds passed, it was enough time for her to look at him, for him to register the confusion and helplessness in her eyes. That look sat in their adult relationship; it existed there beneath the extreme courteousness with which he treated her. Elizabeth. Every now and then it came back to him, her child's figure, so tinged and outlined with the fear he felt, so shaded and blurred by the door about to shut, so colored and made radiant by panic. He was startled by the grace he had never seen, would never see again, in his sister. He had not gotten a clear look. You can't see correctly in that situation. Your eyes do not have time to get used to and take in what you are seeing. It was pressed into his memory; a photograph before there were photographs. To such an extent that he later wrote to a mother of small girls who tended toward running around scantily clad: "For the sake of their little brother I quite think you may find it desirable to bring such habits to an end after this summer. A boy's head soon imbibes precocious ideas which might be a cause of unhappiness in future years. . . ."

In the distance he could see the familiar spires rising up against pearl sky.

15

Hunt was eating dinner by himself, cold mutton on a chipped plate with a pattern of cabbage roses and a bottle of claret, reading the draft of *Alice's Adventures under Ground*. Dodgson had tossed the manuscript on his desk as he was leaving that afternoon. A children's story, he had said.

The dedication page was written in large careful letters entwined with leaves: *In Memory of a Summer Day*. How odd to put it that way, Hunt thought. In memory of. As if the day, the summer, the people involved, had died.

Hunt had told Dodgson how much he admired the photographs of Alice Liddell. Dodgson seemed pleased. And no further conversation ensued.

Hunt turned the pages while he ate. He could feel the violent charm running through the story. The playing-card gardeners are painting the white roses red. They are afraid of the queen's arbitrary authority. Off with his head. The queen arrives, with soldiers carrying clubs and courtiers ornamented in diamonds. All of this out of a deck of playing cards.

One minute Alice is playing croquet with a mallet made of an ostrich who keeps twisting its head to look up at her, and the next she is watching a gryphon dance a lobster quadrille. Hunt thought to himself how strange the story was on so many levels, that religiously adamant Dodgson would mock moralism. That regulation-obsessed Dodgson would write so bitingly about rules themselves. That someone as orderly as Dodgson would so irreverently approach the issue of logical progression. That someone who was so proper and correct in every way would write a book about the utter breakdown of the rational world. Where did the story come from, then?

A whole other man existed in Dodgson: a wild, chatty, affectionate, flamboyantly deranged man with a very tangential relationship to the solid world. Hunt had sensed this submerged personality, occasionally seen it dimly and in flashes. But now in the pages before him was the passport documenting his existence. And yet, perhaps the contradictions made sense. The rules inspired and reassured and flowed through Dodgson like wind through a windmill, giving him energy. And it was precisely his seriousness about the rules that made him qualified to comment on them, to turn against them so effectively.

Hunt noticed a small grease stain on the corner of a page. He rubbed it off with his jacket sleeve until it was barely noticeable.

What interested Hunt was the flow of the thing, its speech: transitions abruptly done away with, subject shifts fantastically smooth. He saw the stutterer skipping the difficult word; employing a creative approach to language, simply hopping over a line when it skipped and gave him trouble. The story moved so quickly, and yet it moved in its own way. Graceful and fantastical and seamless and brilliant, snakelike and clever, and yet not how things really were for Dodgson in life.

Hunt had a sip of wine. He came to the trial. The story collects there like rain in a ditch. Someone has stolen the jam tarts. The atmosphere is wild and grave. The queen wants the sentence before the evidence. And Alice sweetly objects, *You can't have the sentence before the trial*. Everything is backward. You are nothing but a pack of cards, Alice says, and then they all fly at her, and she screams, and it is only a dream, and leaves are falling gently on her head. Hunt was surprised to feel himself perspire. The terror so delicate and realistic. Like the tiny leaves in the drawing.

Alice. Hunt felt as if he was beginning to know her, to feel Dodgson's affection for her. Spending so much effort to entertain a single child, not your own, was certainly out of the ordinary. And then there was a devotion in the photographs. Dodgson had forged a friendship with the girl. She must be a muse of some sort. Inspiring and provoking and coaxing this story out of him. But Hunt was not satisfied. There was something more. But he didn't know what it was. The feeling made him jittery. Falling off a cliff, like one of the pages of Dodgson's story. Turning it and realizing you were in a whole different place, on a beach with a mock turtle capering wildly across the sand.

It was quite extraordinary, Hunt thought, leafing back to the drawing of Alice's small head balanced on a long, long stalklike neck. He thought of Dodgson's early-morning visit, his frantic silence. *You can't have the sentence before the trial.*

The maid cleared the dishes. She left the nearly empty wineglass. Hunt sat at the table in silence.

⚶

June 18, 1863

Please God Give me a new heart.

⚶

"Dr. Hunt." Mrs. Liddell cornered him next to the sandwiches. "How lovely to see you again."

He bowed politely. With her dark hair pulled back in loose waves, diamonds glittering in her ears, and dark brown, gold-flecked eyes, she had a sort of gypsy-style prettiness. Her presence reminded him of how little contact he had with women these days.

"I've heard of your work with the stutter," she said. "And I wondered if you had ever seen our Mr. Dodgson."

"I am acquainted with him."

"He's a great friend of ours," she said.

"Yes?"

"Or perhaps I should say of our children. He is the cleverest storyteller I have ever encountered. He has absolutely enchanted us."

Dr. Hunt swallowed a bite of butter sandwich. He had been enjoying the party until this conversation with the dean's wife. She had said nothing uncomplimentary about Dodgson, but something in her tone made him uncomfortable.

He saw one of Dodgson's photographs of Alice on the side table next to the wax gardenias under their glass dome. Staring out at him.

"He has been spending quite a lot of time around our middle daughter, Alice, photographing her," Mrs. Liddell went on. "All of the girls, really."

Everywhere he looked he saw little ovals and rectangles filled with Alice.

"His photographs seem rather good."

"Yes, as you can see we are quite spoiled."

She was leaning so close to him he could isolate the honeysuckle in her perfume.

"He almost seems to prefer childish company to that of his peers." She smiled. "Fortunate for them, I suppose."

"Who can comb the depths of the artistic temperament, my dear lady?" And with that he made his excuses and drifted into the crowd in the direction of the brandy and soda.

Mrs. Liddell stared after him, feeling misunderstood. But she was wrong. He had understood her perfectly.

June 20, 1863

I set up the tripod slowly, suddenly old & weak & doddering. The light against the red sofa, with its swirling Japanese flowers. Alice is leaning back, chewing on her hair. She bends down & removes one of her boots.

There are times when one cannot see—the scene unfolding does not take form in the mind's eye—a thick dust coating the lens—

The moments are knit together. How I cannot say.

*Like an old Tiresias the rest of my senses rise to
take the place of sight: The draft in the room—The soft
rosewood of camera against hands—The taste of tea—
The smell of collodion in the air—A blind man stumbling through the familiar.*

*I turn away. Outside, the sun is filtering through
trees, diamonds of shadow & light trembling on the
lawn. I can feel her limbs in motion, feel her shaking off
the last undergarments, even though I am halfway
across the room facing a different direction.*

*Suddenly Dr. Hunt's line runs absurdly through my
mind—tell the bewilderingly bad boy dinner is delicious.*

*And then I turn & look—through the camera—eye
through lens—It is the crushed glass that sees her—
cradling her image in its crystal depths. The room
shakes in my hands & then falls into place. The camera
can see what I cannot—enacts my vision and releases
me—*

*And then I see her, a pearly perfect stretch of Alice,
heavenlike and . . . No, let me say for once what I truly
see: delicate olive-tinted skin, a purplish bruise rimmed
with green on her thigh, two tiny swells, a stomach
slightly protruding, a red crease where her undergarments pressed into her stomach, ribs outlined, black
eyes staring defiantly at the camera. As God designed
her. Mirabile dictu.*

16

Alice ran through the garden, tears streaming down her face. Her mother looked up from the dahlias; caught her by the upper arms, and demanded to know what was wrong. But Alice couldn't answer through the choke of tears, even if she knew.

The pain was equivalent to a bone breaking. The pain was about one's whole bodily structure cracking and then being knit together again in another form. They were the tears of transformation. Like the "eat me, drink me" kind of growing in Dodgson's story where Alice takes a bite of something and grows into a giant, it was bizarre and sudden and out of control. Alice hardly knows who she is. *Being so many different sizes in one day is very confusing,* she says to the caterpillar. *When you have to turn into a chrysalis . . . and then after that into a butterfly, I should think you'll feel it a little queer. And* that was the pain, the wrenching of who you were into who you will be. The tearing apart of one being into another. The force and violence of that change was making her cry.

Alice shook loose of her mother and ran up the stairs to her room and slammed the door. She was crying so hard she was having trouble getting air.

She had seen her naked self in the oval mirror in Dodgson's room. A partial sideways sliver of her nakedness flew at her and startled her: Alice undressing for a man.

The room tilts. She is standing in a pool of cotton. Stepping out of her dress. The moment sprayed with color, the deep crimson of the sofa, the melted candy color of the sky, the bright turquoise of the rug. Her legs feel like twigs; her body, delicate, papery, like a leaf.

She thinks of crawling into his lap, safely there, on his knees again, her head against his chest. *But wait a bit, the oyster cried, before we have our chat. For some of us are out of breath and all of us are fat.*

The air is cool on her skin. In the corner, standing neatly next to the sofa, she sees the small fawn-colored boots, with buttons down the side, that her mother had brought her from London. Her arm is folded across her chest, and then down by her side. His eyes on her. Eyes across skin. The damp look she has seen before. She is peeled open. Her mother brought her those boots last week, small replicas of her own. The boots make her sad. The cold is surrounding her now. Her hands are on her thighs. Her stomach feels funny. The whole room is drawn into her, wood floors, fireplace, white ceiling. The fear, clarifying and electric, in front of the camera. The look in the strange familiar eyes, suddenly terrifying; like goblins chewing mangoes, pears, plums, melons. She is stuck there like pit inside plump fruit.

She feels the wet on her cheeks. Dissolving the moment, making it into something she could understand.

Through it all she felt an emerging loveliness. A new being sprouting fully formed like Athena out of the head of Zeus. Her skin satin. The light caught in her hair. A crown of flowers. The beauty she had not known was there. Running through her the pleasure of his looking; not his attraction to her, her attraction to herself.

She stood differently, aware of his watching her. The tears were an unloosing of something in herself she had never felt. An overflowing of feeling that she could not put into words. She had no control at all over the tears, just like the situation that unraveled in Dodgson's rooms. She stood in front of him, feeling the excitement rising through her body, the luxury of being appreciated, the fear, and then—there was something else. She was waiting, without knowing precisely for what, and she felt it—the waiting—in every muscle. The tightness coiled up in her, the newness of standing there naked and goose-pimpled, feet in rough rug, backs of calves rubbing against worn satin sofa, feeling every brush against every surface differently than she had before, his gray eyes on her; it was desire, more than anything else, that was making her cry.

Later that evening, Edith stood in the doorway with a silver tray of milk and sandwiches. She had persuaded Miss Prickett to let her bring the tray in, because she wanted to get closer, to enter the inner sanctum of this wild and showy grief.

But now she hesitated on the threshold. Her mother had tried to talk to Alice earlier, but Alice turned her head to the wall and refused to speak. *What happened? Nothing. What happened? Nothing.*

Edith, listening in the hallway, found this chorus hard to believe. Alice trying to deflect attention? Alice not basking in the drama of a story extracted from her piece by piece? Alice saying nothing?

"What happened?" Edith asked softly, walking toward the bed.

"Nothing," Alice said. Her head sideways on white pillow. Her eyelids swollen. Frog eyes, Edith thought.

She put the tray down on the night table and sat on the edge of the bed.

Alice lifted up her head and reached for the glass of milk. As the arm of her nightgown slipped back, her wrist looked thin. Her hair was staticky and stuck to the side of her face.

Edith knew Alice hadn't eaten since breakfast and knew she must be hungry, but she wouldn't do something as mundane as consuming a bite of food in front of her sister.

"Are you ill?" Edith asked. She felt bad for Alice, or she felt bad for not feeling bad.

"No."

"Tell me what happened. I promise I shall keep it to myself."

"Edie, please," Alice said. "Leave me alone."

"Alice, I—"

"Nothing happened," Alice said.

It came to her suddenly how she and Alice used to play

wedding in the garden when they were younger. How Alice would always get to be the bride, with roses in her hair, walking down the aisle, and Edith would always have to be the groom. They would recite their wedding vows, press their lips together as hard as they could, and collapse into hysterical laughter. The kind of laughter that made it hard to breathe.

"Edie, please."

Edith slipped out of the room and closed the door. Once in the wedding game she and Alice had touched tongues. They were both startled by the hideousness of the feeling and immediately stepped back. She had no idea what possessed them to do it. That was the last time she felt their separateness so strongly.

⚜

The stones of the university were disappearing into green. Everything looked overgrown, shaggy, the azaleas, the hedges, the rosebushes, the surprising pocket of yellow wildflowers bursting up from behind the gate, the ivy and vines crawling up the walls. The heat only increased the disintegrating aspect of the place, the sense that the soft buildings were crumbling into all of this lushness, being reclaimed by the earth.

When Dodgson knocked on the door, Miss Prickett let him in and told him that Alice was unwell.

He could not let this misunderstanding, which was how he looked at it, grow up and blossom between him and Alice. He wanted to give her copies of the photographs, three nudes, one of her sitting on the sofa, one of her lying on a fur throw on the floor, one of her standing. He planned to paint a seashell as the background of one of them, a nymph emerging from the sea, and then transpose it. But he hadn't had time since the evening before.

He walked up the stairs, through the upstairs gallery toward her room. He tried to call up her face, but for the first time he couldn't. Her nakedness in his studio had seemed like it would never end, the minutes slow and syrupy, time itself thickening and holding them there. Sunlight, nut-colored skin, sofa. Then suddenly she broke through the mood; she cried.

When Alice sat down on the floor of his room and pulled on her stockings, tears pouring soundlessly down her face, he had not known what to say. He had been disoriented by her crying, as if he were caught in one of his dreams and was not called on to act, simply to stand by and wait for it to pass. So he let her run. Afterward he tried to reassure himself. What could he have said?

He stood in the center of his room for a long time without moving, the wind rustling through the large heart-shaped leaves of the grapevines outside his window. He didn't want to run after her, he wanted to run after the moment she had taken with her.

He felt an unaccustomed suspense when he developed the photographs. He had watched the corners of the plate disappear under the chemicals. What would they show? It was almost too much to appear on the glass plate, the moment filled with too much, but then there she was. Still a child. A beguiling, beautiful child. A child on the precipice, but a child nonetheless. After she left, he had washed and dried his hands, put the stoppers on the chemicals, put the bottles and glass measure and funnel back in the cabinet. He had convinced himself that this was the kind of squabble he could smooth over, a minor ripple in the surface.

He was sure that when she saw the photographs she would understand. She could not fail to be moved by the photographs.

The photographs were what *she* wanted. He was sure of it. He was there. He had felt it in the room. He had not misunderstood. That was part of the beauty he witnessed. A kind of voluntary unfolding.

Looking at the photographs, he felt for the first time that he was in the presence of something sacred. There poised in front of him was the impossible convergence of opposites, the logical contradictions that had intrigued him about art for as long as he could remember: she was naked but not naked; it was illicit but not illicit; he had her but didn't have her. He had found the place that came before dreams and after life. And for him that was part of the perfection: a half-developed fantasy. He wanted nothing more than to stand there and look at her. He had never known that state: wanting nothing more. He was enthralled.

Now he was standing at the door of her room. She was in a thin, white nightgown, propped up on her pillows, pale and radiant and miserable-looking.

"I'm s-s-sorry that you are ill."

She looked disgusted.

"We w-w-w-won't—"

"L-l-l-leave me alone," she said meanly.

"Alice." He ran his hand along her white nubby bedspread. "I'm sorry."

Her uneven hair was stuck to her face.

"No," said Alice. "Stop."

His stammer was giving him away. He wasn't sorry.

He wasn't sure she wanted him to be sorry.

She was forcing him to lie to her; she was dividing them from each other; she was dividing them from what they both knew.

Dodgson was aware that his mind was moving slowly. He felt like he was barely able to understand what was going on around him, like the dullest student; it was taking him that long to get to his thoughts.

He didn't know how long he sat there in silence on the chair next to Alice's bed.

The slamming of the door downstairs jolted them both. Mrs. Liddell. Dodgson put the photographs in Alice's hand, put his hand on hers, curled her fingers around them, and then hurried out of the room, down the back stairs into the kitchen, whispering a quick thank you to Miss Prickett as he put on his hat and closed the back door.

Alice pulled the bedspread around her shoulders like a cape, listening to the padded sound of his footsteps disappearing down the hallway. She lay with the pillow between her knees. Her worn nightgown soft against her skin. She did not think to herself: I never want to see him again.

Ch. Ch.
Sunday Night
Dear Mrs. Liddell,
Thank you very much for your kind invitation—I
am going to ask you to be so very kind as to excuse me:

but I cannot explain why properly tonight (it is very
late), nor tomorrow as I am going to London for the
day—After that I will try to write it—
    Believe me,
    Sincerely yours,
       C. L. Dodgson

Edith periodically rifled through both of her sisters' things. She never found anything interesting, except Lorina's diary, which she read regularly, mostly about rocks and young men with flashing eyes, but the search itself gave her a feeling of furtive closeness. The next morning she was going through Alice's dollhouse, her keepsake album, with its bits of dried rose petals falling to the floor, her miniature ivory chess set, her Indian elephant with tiny mirrors stitched to its saddle, her doll with the shiny black face, the pillow she'd half embroidered with a cat and then abandoned. Edith swept her arm under the bed. There was nothing but dust balls, cat hair, and crumpled pieces of paper. Her dress was getting dirty from kneeling on the floor, which would have disturbed her if she hadn't been so absorbed.

Out the window she could see Alice listlessly walking through the garden. Her mother had insisted that she go out for a walk. She had been inside for two and a half days and the air would do her good.

Alice disappeared beneath the branches of the oak. Edith and Alice used to spend hours with the trees. They would run up and throw their arms around each tree—willow, oak, small maple—and pretend each one was gossiping and telling them secrets, a buzzing village of trees. When they came home they would have bits of bark and leaves in their hair.

Edith continued the search methodically. She found a pocket knife, a ball of yellow wool her mother had been searching for, and a dusty pencil drawing of two fat twins from Mr. Dodgson. There was something soothing about going through Alice's things. She looked at the miniature wrought-iron doll's bed in the corner. Wasn't Alice too old for dolls? When she was eleven she did not intend to have dolls in her room. Dolls created entirely the wrong impression. She was already feeling a little old for dolls. She reached under the thin mattress and felt several stiff pieces of paper. What were they? They weren't there the week before. She drew them out.

And then she saw: Alice not wearing any clothes. A sight she had seen before countless times in less startling contexts. She had the same longish nose and lank, dark brown hair, but her body looked unusually graceful and grown up. She had tiny puffs around her nipples. *Alice sans habillement*. Edith was proud of this piece of French vocabulary summoned under duress. She wished someone was there to hear it. She had never seen a naked photograph, and frankly it had not occurred to her that such a thing could exist. Photographs were something you fussed over, dressed up for, adjusted ribbons and hair for. Which made Alice staring up at her, completely bare and divested of her secret, all the more shocking.

Edith ran her hand along the matte surface of the photographs. For a second she thought she had made them up.

And then the thought whipped through her. All this time she had thought that there was something wrong with her, and now she saw that there was something wrong with *Alice*. She felt redeemed, lifted out of the jealousy she had inhabited for so long: if this is what Mr. Dodgson's friendship meant, then it was never worth having. She knew there was no way on earth or heaven that she would ever take all her clothes off for Mr. Dodgson or anyone else.

Vaguely, she understood that Alice would not be able to get married now and live respectably. Her name would be whispered at dinner tables—"And have you heard what happened to poor Alice Liddell . . ."; she would be one of the hushed and forbidden subjects that flashed through the surface of polite conversation like colored ribbons in a girl's hair. Alice would be the sister they never spoke of. She would leave the deanery. Edith was not sure, but she thought Alice might have to become an actress.

Edith was lost in the magnitude of her discovery. She propped the photographs on the bed and made them dance.

She stood up, lifted her dress, tucked the pictures into her petticoat, not caring that the edges were cutting into her stomach, and carefully closed the door.

17

Mrs. Liddell stood in the dark-wood-paneled dining room, holding open the curtain. The sky was bright blue with strips of cloud. Lord Newry was sitting on the wrought-iron bench, legs crossed, hat on the grass, Lorina and Edith next to him in cotton dresses, parasols leaning against the tree. Lorina was laughing. He would probably marry Lorina if she wanted him to. There was a satisfaction in this. Directing the flow of attraction, rising above and controlling it. She used to love riding a horse through the field behind her parents' house in Sussex. She had a little of that feeling now, the horse under her, long grass.

She drifted back inside to contemplate the floral centerpiece for a dinner party that night, blue globes of hydrangea. Her husband sat at the table, leafing through his mail.

"Alice is still in bed," said Mrs. Liddell, taking a violent clip, a puffy blue flower falling to the table.

Two days had passed and the servants were talking about her condition, which made Mrs. Liddell uneasy. At first she had thought Alice was just in a particularly theatrical mood, but the longer it staggered on, like the last act of a Shakespeare tragedy, characters bleeding on the floor, the more worried she became. She knew when she sat on the edge of her daughter's bed that she was in the presence of something more than a mood.

She went through the menu in her mind: lobster bisque, asparagus, potatoes, cauliflower gratin, filet de soles, roast quarter of lamb, scallops of chicken, neopolitan cakes, cherry water ices. Had she remembered to tell the cook to buy coffee?

"We should consider the doctor," the dean said. "If this continues, that is. Shall I call him now?"

"Perhaps you might wait until tomorrow," Mrs. Liddell said. "I don't want." She paused. "The party."

She wondered if the lamb had been a mistake. The last time it had been dry.

"I know what happened," said Edith, who was poking the cat with a twig on the floor beneath the table.

The dean looked as surprised as if the centerpiece itself was about to offer up a theory.

"What then?" her mother asked, absently plucking off a handful of blue petals. She hadn't remembered the coffee. She would have to tell the cook.

Without saying anything, Edith slipped out from under the table and put the photographs in front of her mother.

Mrs. Liddell picked them up.

She saw the expanse of stomach, silver in the light. Flesh of her. She remembered, such narrow thighs, such thin arms, the swing blowing in the wind, blue dress billowing. The rags that had been there before and were not now. Slipped off. The way Miss Prickett must have wandered off after she dropped Alice for the photographs. The way she had seen her from the back in the kitchen, gossiping with the cook when she was supposed to be with Alice in Dodgson's rooms. Her bonnet hanging around her neck. Steam from the soup blurring the air. The way Dodgson had once written her, early on, *Would you kindly tell me if your girls are invitable singly, or in sets only, like the circulating-library novels?* The violin shape of her daughter on her side. Her own shame laid out for everyone to see.

"Edith," Mrs. Liddell said, "I must have a word with your father."

Dodgson had the photographs he had taken of eleven-year-old Alice Jane Donkin fanned out in front of him. He had written on the back of each one, *The Elopement.* He had first met Alice Jane through her uncle William Fishburn Donkin, who was an astronomy professor at the university. His younger brother Wilfred had been quite taken with her. And Dodgson had done the whole set of elopement pictures at her parents' house at Barmby Moor last October. They were the most elaborately posed photographs he had ever taken. The girl was balanced outside her open bedroom window on the second floor, walking down a rope ladder. One of the most challenging poses he had ever attempted. She clutched the side of the window, a hooded cape over long curly hair, white dress puffing out beneath her. He had worried the whole time that she would fall. The ladder shook in the wind. The clouds gathered. She looked down. Her face milk white. Her terrier was barking down below and wouldn't stop, irritating him, making it hard to concentrate. The lace of her petticoat showed under her dress. Her black shoe reaching for the next rung of rope. *I am not afraid*, she called down. Her voice surprisingly loud and composed. She was not afraid. The scruffy dog ran around his ankles. The upward funnel of petticoat was too visible. He stepped back. His feet crunching dried leaves. And took the picture. He had intended it to be humorous, of course, a kind of *Northanger Abbey* in photographs, a send-up of romances. But the rough, mottled texture of the bricks in the side of the house was too clear, too detailed in the frame of the photograph, and it was hard to keep track of the fantasy. They were right there, girl climbing out of window to meet her lover, suitcases packed in the carriage. The sound of her parents' disapproval rustling through the trees. There was something haunting about her expression too, a concentration, as if she really was stealing away from her parents, and there also, in the tautness of her muscles, in the reaching down of white-stockinged ankle, the dangle of shoe, her desire to escape. Afterward they both were exhausted. He gave her chocolate biscuits and ginger beer, which they voraciously consumed on the grass.

Mrs. Liddell swept through Alice's room and tore up all the letters Charles Dodgson had sent to her daughter. She shook open each book on Alice's bookshelf to make sure that every last one fluttered into her hands.

Of course, it was possible that Alice had no idea what she was doing in the photographs, and yet, there was a look in her eyes, a play with the camera, smoky, teasing. There was an upward turn at the edges of her mouth, which could have been a look-at-the-camera smile. But under the circumstances, naked in front of a grown man, that seemed unlikely.

She held up one letter that was written backward and meant to be deciphered in a mirror. Why all of these codes? They were codes that anyone under the sun would be able to decipher, and yet, they added intrigue to the childish exchange. They added unnecessary intrigue.

I send you 1/two millionth of a kiss, she read to herself. 1/two millionth of a kiss! What kind of man divides a kiss into two millionths, she thought, as she tore the purple-inked page into pieces. He is not even a man, he is 1/two millionth of a man. It's the single most depraved thing I have ever encountered, she thought, trying to hide himself behind geometry. And his reasoning is so transparent for a supposedly brilliant man. A kiss is bad. A two millionth of a kiss is simply charming. He thinks he is not accountable for anything he says cleverly. But as far as she was concerned he was more accountable for the things he said cleverly.

A whole woman is too much for him, she thought. 3/8ths of a woman is not. Of all the young men who gathered around her, who flirted with her and flattered her, innocently and harmlessly of course, Dodgson stood apart. She felt his distance from her, and worse.

She was used to walking in to a party and feeling men's eyes on her, not in the way she had when she was younger, of course, but feeling them drawn to her nonetheless. In Oxford circles, she was still a beauty, still a presence. Dodgson resisted her the way other young men didn't; he wouldn't let her take him over, claim him, mother him. As she reached her late thirties her seductive powers had merged with a kind of motherly warmth, making her hold over men if anything stronger. But she could feel how little he admired her.

She shook out another letter. *Thank you for sending your poor busy old friend two million hugs and kisses. But I couldn't go on hugging and kissing more than 12 hours a day, and I wouldn't like to spend Sundays that way. So you see it would take 23 weeks' hard work. Really, my dear child, I cannot spare the time.* She had a quick image of herself, flushed, at around twelve, at her parents' dinner table, talking ardently about poetry to a young curate, over raspberry tart, and then her daughter's eyes looking out from the photograph.

Mrs. Liddell opened all of the drawers of Alice's cupboard, looking for any notes or drawings that might be concealed.

Another bundle was hidden among the petticoats. She didn't try to read any of them; after the infinitesimal fraction of a kiss, and millions of hugs, she'd had enough of Mr. Dodgson's inner landscape for one day. She simply tore them into strips, and then squares, and then let them fall, purple- and cream-colored diamonds, to the ground. She didn't care about the mess. The maid would sweep them up later. For once she didn't care what the maid thought.

Her anger at Dodgson hid another, deeper anger, which was at Alice herself. Respectable children did not pose for naked portraits. Her anger at Alice seared the lining of her stomach and kept her up all night; it sat with her, all the time, like an incessantly chattering parrot, and eventually turned against her. She remembered the tiny head that could fit in her palm like a large orange. What kind of mother would allow something like this to happen to her child?

Alice watched from the bed, not bothering to lift up her head from her knees. The air was still. The room was stifling. She noticed that leaves of the right-side-up flowers on her wallpaper were entwined, as if they were holding hands, with the leaves of the upside-down ones. It was only as her mother searched angrily through her drawers that Alice knew she had been hiding something.

18

That night Mrs. Liddell carefully lifted the sheets, climbed out of bed, and felt around with her feet for her slippers, without waking her husband. She could feel the draft on her bare legs. She could tell from the color of the sky that it was after midnight. She never slept deeply. Some portion of her mind was always alert. Right now, there was more of a feeling of disturbance than an actual noise, and her first thought was that it was the baby in the nursery, but Miss Prickett would have heard her if she had woken up. Her next thought was that it was one of the girls, probably Alice, tiptoe-ing down the hallway. She was already composing a speech to Miss Prickett about how it was also her responsibility to look after the older girls at night and make sure they stayed in their wing of the house. This was really too much. Alice was not a child anymore. She had to stop tolerating this sort of behavior.

She had to make the rules stick. She couldn't let Alice's will dictate and tyrannize the entire family. The photograph flashed through her mind, skin white and private as the inside of a seashell. Her household was becoming disorderly, was virtually falling apart stone by stone, and it was her own fault.

She got up and lit a candle, her hand over the flame.

Then, out the window, she saw a slender male figure moving catlike through the gray garden toward the back door.

She would have been afraid had the man not seemed so insubstantial and almost, in the way he moved, apologetic.

Her eyes adjusted to darkness, and the situation began to take form.

Dodgson froze when he saw her in the window. As if by not moving any closer he could take back all of the movements of the past ten minutes and be back in his room.

Alice's mother looked different in her white nightgown, softer. He couldn't get over how different she looked.

It was a strange intimacy to be thrown into with her, partially clothed, in the soft yellow light. Her thick black hair fell down her shoulders in waves. Her face looked smooth in the shadows. She seemed undone. A disheveled, unfinished version of herself. For a moment he thought there was a chance that she might understand. He thought he might be able to talk to her for the first time.

He looked at her helplessly.

And then he turned and ran back through the deanery garden. The sharp silhouettes of the lilies rose up in the moonlight. It felt good to be running. He wished he could run away, and not just from the deanery.

Of course he never would have gone through with it. He realized almost immediately that he was not really going to steal Alice away. If he had made it to her room he would have watched her sleep and then left. He didn't even *want* to take her away. The idea was all that his addled brain could produce. A solution in the practical world, or so it seemed at the time. This is the sort of thing he came up with when he let the chalk stray from the blackboard.

He thought for a moment of the puppet theater he had made at the rectory when he was ten and the scenes he played out for the amusement of his sisters. Creeping through the darkness, running off in the dead of the night. More suited to the puppet theater than the solemn spires of Christ Church. *The Elopement.* He couldn't remember what he had been thinking. He had never meant the money in his bureau drawer to take him to France. France was just the idea of someplace else. He had dutifully packed his large suitcase, white flannel trousers, straw hat, waistcoats, shirts, white and black bow ties. But as always, there was the great gaping hole in his plan, a kind of frenetic blackness at its very center: when he was settled with Alice in a small brick house in the French countryside, shaded on one side by grapevines that twisted through a trellis, what were they going to do? He wanted to *want* to run away with Alice, but he did not. When it came down to it, he did not. The sad part was how capable he was of love, how his love was all there, laid out for him, a house entirely set up and furnished, and yet he couldn't live in it. He turned the key and rattled it in the difficult lock.

Alice lay under her covers replaying the afternoon in Dodgson's rooms, the small mound of clothing on the floor, the boots by the sofa, the glare of sunlight through window. She was caught in that afternoon like a fly frozen in amber. She felt the warmth spread through her legs, along with an opening up, a vista, like turning a corner and seeing a view of the mountains you hadn't known was there: Alice, Princess of Denmark, Alice Ruskin, Lady Alice Newry.

19

Hunt bent down over his small washbasin and rinsed his face with cold water. It had been a long day. Then he took the photographs of Alice that Mrs. Liddell had given him and spread them out on his desk. He couldn't focus properly at the deanery with Mrs. Liddell scanning his face for minute changes of expression, and so he had taken them home to think.

Now Hunt saw everything; he saw the longing and the hint of melancholy, how could he not? Somehow Dodgson managed to get himself into the photographs. One could not avoid his thoughts. They were right there, wistful and furious and sepia-toned. For some reason the dark greenish color added an additional layer of illicitness to the pictures. Making the bare, clinical images seem dreamlike and otherworldly. Beyond your grasp but in it. Pretty and scientific, all at once.

The girl looked so young.

Hunt thought he should have seen the faint shadow of the naked child in the earlier series of photographs. He should have been able to isolate and anticipate the precise nature of Dodgson's interest. And then he realized it was even worse. He *had* seen it. He had seen how the girl had inspired Dodgson. He felt the love in the photographs, in the story *Alice's Adventures*, in the confusing fall down the rabbit hole, and not known what to do with it. What *did* one do with it?

He found it impossible to say, even a relatively open-minded man like himself, that these photographs were simply art for art's sake.

He had seen a nude photograph of children before. He remembered one, several naked children seen from the back playing around a large stone by the ocean. But it was nothing like this. The sugariness saved it from prurience. The children were younger than Alice, and coyly obscured. Cupids playing in water. No, Dodgson's portraits were something else entirely.

They were the kind of photographs that did not stand on their own. They bled into the world around them. They suggested; they evoked; they forced the imagination into strange positions. One couldn't help but feel the story unfolding behind the picture, how he got her to stand like that, how she pulled off her dress with the single careless gesture of a child, how Dodgson took it off the floor and threw it on the sofa, or folded it, Dodgson would probably fold, how he adjusted her hair so it just grazed her collarbone. . . . He wanted to stop the pictures but he couldn't.

There was, in the photographs, a strange beauty of contrasts, so childlike and knowing, so elusive it offers a man a hide-and-seek with himself: maybe this is not lust, maybe it is just the innocent frolic of a child stepping out of a bath. The exact truth cannot be pinned down because the truth is not there. The truth is somewhere in between. The truth is whatever you want it to be, because the little girl is not old enough to know how she feels.

Hunt leafed through the photographs again.

Her legs were beautiful, her thighs so long and narrow. They were almost like a woman's but then not at all like a woman's. The play of difference, so close and yet not at all close, was what made them so alluring. It was almost comic the structure of little girls' beauty: so near to an adult woman's beauty and yet so crucially far. Like one of Dodgson's puns. In one of the photographs she was lying on a thick fur throw with her hips swiveled toward the camera. She seemed like she was opening herself to the stare.

The slit looked so bare and exposed there. Velvety, peach-like. The pictures had the power to pull you in. You could not help being drawn into the sensual sway. As if the whole world were compressed between the rug and sofa on the second floor of the old library building of Christ Church. There was something tyrannical about these images that would not allow any other way of looking. That was what horrified Hunt the most, and he could only imagine how Mrs. Liddell must have felt.

The danger of this sort of fantasy was that it imposed itself on you. Creating new avenues and channels that you had not known existed in yourself. Hunt wished the picture did not exist. He wished he had never seen this little girl standing naked, knee bent, foot pressed against the wall.

He wanted to rescue Alice, to throw a blanket around her

and sweep her back to the day before these photographs were taken. This man should be run out of Oxford, should not live near any decent family.

And then the man himself intruded on the sermon that was forming in Hunt's head. Dodgson, gentle, soft-spoken, stuttering Dodgson. He thought of his long, carefully combed, curling hair, and the unlikely, endearing vanity it betrayed. Could Dodgson be anything but harmless?

He had witnessed the struggle. He knew that Dodgson tried to keep all of this to himself, to withdraw, to the point where he actually swallowed parts of words. It suddenly occurred to him that Dodgson could have no idea what the photographs meant. He may have been thinking fairies and nymphs, thinking gossamer and shimmer, thinking, who knows, the Royal Academy of Art and Dante Gabriel Rossetti's "Bocca Baciata" without thinking about how these three pieces of paper could compromise the girl's future.

And yet they were the most eloquent representation the doctor had thus far encountered of Dodgson's true self: the man watching in awe. The man on the periphery of his own longing. The rich desire that flooded the photographs like sunlight.

What an entanglement, Hunt thought. With the dean's wife on one hand and the shy mathematical lecturer on the other. He was caught between the two of them, truly and inextricably caught. He wished there was a way he could honorably drop Dodgson.

Everyone had secrets. Hunt thought of his own, of the prostitute he had seen in London, walking down Haymarket, red hair wavy, falling long and unruly. He remembered following her up a flight of stairs to her rooms, the short, passionate interlude there, and then of the disease he may very well have passed on to his malformed child.

He did not usually allow himself to return to this memory; in fact he did not usually remember it at all. The painful symptoms, the pretending the painful symptoms did not exist, the connection as definite as the train tracks back to London. She had been so lovely. Shaking the bangles on her arms so they jingled. So uncomplicated. So different from his wife, who turned toward the wall at night, holding a pillow to her stomach. She had the faintest lisp when she asked him to wash himself beforehand. In a porcelain basin balanced on a chair.

She was the answer to a prayer he did not know he had made.

And he had gone back. He had gotten used to the basin, used to ignoring the risk of disease.

The hidden layer of life comes out, not usually in a photograph of course, but somehow. Desire never fails to haunt you, to come back to you and reproach you in another form. And how could he blame Dodgson? How could he *think* of blaming Dodgson? He himself had managed through a few carnal tussles, a few insignificant evenings in a narrow third-floor flat on a little street off Haymarket, to destroy something that did not yet exist. Hunt thought of how many weaknesses there are, how inefficiently made the human spirit was. He thought of Dodgson stuttering, and eating so little his shirt collar was loose around his neck, and burning his hand, however he managed that. One can never underestimate the chaos and cruelty of nature, and, he caught himself thinking, of God.

Hunt got up and put on his overcoat, slipped the

photographs in his pocket, and walked quickly down the narrow hallway.

Dodgson held Mrs. Liddell's note in his hands. There were branches of pain in his chest. He was not going to see Alice.

This is a feeling that will never again be replicated: the loss of. The unexplained disappearance of. The murder of.

He held the scalloped page and sank into the loops and coils of midnight blue. He was falling past the words, reaching out to catch hold of them. The only solid thing he had to hold in his hands. *No longer desirable for you to spend time with our family.*

Over the past few days it had been hard for him to tell what was real. The fantasies of taking Alice off to France had dissolved, leaving behind a slightly sordid feeling, like a posh hotel room after the guests leave, blankets strewn across the bed, balled-up paper on the desk, sheets crumpled on the floor. He recognized the fantasy as sheer desperation. How to prolong the ambiguity, how to carry it away with him, since things had become so impossible for him here.

He wanted to stop feeling this way; he wanted to stop feeling. The soreness in his chest. The loss, infinite and silky and terrifying as the sky. But what could he do? He looked around the room. It was then he remembered the amber bottle of laudanum in the back of his cabinet behind his razor. He took it out and smelled the stopper. He looked into the bottle.

The liquid was reddish and murky, with a strong, medicinal cherry smell. Was it supposed to have so many little specks and clumps floating in it? Had it gone bad? Did opium go bad?

Dodgson almost decided against it. Finickiness over despair. But he put the drops on his tongue, one after another.

The calm soaked through him. The tension melting. His body softened. The feeling of a mother's palm behind the crown of a baby's head.

He sat on the floor with his back against the wall. He held the bottle with both hands on his lap.

He was separated from his life. He could take it out and put it in a glass case and look at it, as in a museum. Everything was going to be fine.

Tincture of opium, he thought to himself. Tincture. What a strange word. Sometimes familiar words that you use every day sound foreign in your throat, unrecognizable. Like you are visiting your own life, a traveler in your own circumstances. Tinc-ture.

He stood up and walked unsteadily to the window. The sky was violet. The first faint stars were beginning to appear.

The Turkish word for opium drifted into his mind: *Madjoon.* Dodgson grinned at the appropriateness of the term. Mad June.

The words that had seemed so absolute now bent and swayed. *Spend time with our family.* Does that mean he could not touch her hair, does it mean never speak to her again? The words could be taken literally as in physical time, or they could be understood more generally.

His headache was gone. The laudanum worked completely. Sweet nectar of gods. Milk of Paradise. Cherry calm. Every muscle in his body felt relaxed, even more than relaxed, luxurious, imperious, like a king stepping out of a bath. *In Xanadu did Kubla Khan . . .*

He put more drops in his mouth, throwing his head back so they wouldn't trickle down his chin. The peacefulness that a few moments before had seemed so pale and thin and golden, like winter light, suddenly ratcheted up, everything brighter, the reds and browns warmer and richer, the yellows glaring and metallic. His room was suddenly unfamiliar. The serenity more conspicuous now, almost intruding on him. Almost aggressive. Not serenity anymore but euphoria.

In fact, he realized his room was growing larger and larger, the ceilings so high and soaring that they rivaled the cathedral. Church of Dodgson.

The euphoria was exhilarating, but it felt the smallest bit coerced. He felt like someone was putting a hand over his mouth and locking him in a room. He felt like an artificial smile, something else pinned beneath it, trying to get out. In fact, as the feeling developed and grew stronger, it didn't feel much like euphoria at all.

His jaw was hurting. He felt like it was swelling, but when he put his hand to his face, it didn't seem to be. He decided he had better lay down. He spread out on his side on the red sofa, facing the wall.

There was a dampness that was worrying him and nagging at him. That reminded him of disease, of the body rotting and decaying from the inside. He suddenly felt like all of the paint was chipping, the walls literally flaking off, everything seedy and bad-smelling like a rotted tooth.

When Dodgson was a baby he had a bad fever, Infantile Fever, the doctors had called it, and he had lost part of the hearing in one ear. He didn't remember the fever, but he felt wrapped in it now, the heat he couldn't understand, the slow smothering of sound.

Suddenly he was aware of a presence in the room, watching him.

The Mad Hatter was sitting on the foot of the sofa, his thin legs crossed.

"I am afraid I have detected a slight flaw in your story," he said, lighting a cigar, "flowers don't talk. If they do, they are not flowers."

Cigar smoke wafted through the room. His father's deer head sprouted out of the wall in front of him.

"Your dreams are real," the Hatter said. "And your life is—"

He looked into Dodgson's face. "But surely you knew?"

The Hatter was resting his feet on the saucer of a teacup. He rocked the cup with his feet, rattling the dormouse inside.

"I want to sleep," said the mouse crankily, his small body curled against the side of the cup.

"Terribly sorry," the Hatter said. And he spun the cup so quickly and violently the dormouse hit his head on the side of the cup.

Dodgson turned away from them—he wanted to be left alone—and reached for the bottle.

The drops slid down his throat. He had been counting but then he lost count. His stomach felt a tiny bit queasy but it didn't bother him.

Light was flooding in, threatening to wash everything out, to cover it with a blinding paleness. But he could still make out the outline of the Hatter's hat through the luminous smoke.

Dodgson pulled himself to his feet. He needed to get away. How unbearable that he should have to listen to the jabbering of his own fabrications.

He turned and saw the perfectly flat Queen of Hearts sliding through the crack of the closed door. She brushed herself off, adjusted her hair, and loudly pronounced: "Do not. Stop. Do not allow. Do stand up straight. Don't stare. Do not allow your arm to brush against hers. Or his. Wash under. Do not allow. Stop. Off with."

"And the chapter you omitted?" the Hatter said, ignoring her. "How did it begin? *Wrapped in nothing less ethereal than slumber itself?* Not suitable for an eleven-year-old child." He threw back his head and laughed lewdly. "But still I thought you might have left it in."

The Queen of Hearts doubled over and fell flat on the floor. In an instant she writhed into a rug.

"The chapter is in the drawer," the Hatter continued, gesturing to the hall desk. "It's all in the drawer. If you don't believe me you ought to open it and look for yourself."

Dodgson tried to balance himself on the hall desk. He had not written a chapter like that. He pulled open the drawer but it was jammed shut. He shook it but it wouldn't open.

At that point, Humpty Dumpty appeared on his desk, massive and egglike and grotesque, rolls of fat under his chin. He began speaking: "When Alice said to me, 'One can't help growing older,' and I replied, 'One can't but two can. With the proper assistance, you could have left off at seven,' what precisely was the significance of that exchange? Does that mean murder? Does that mean stop her from growing with a knife?"

Humpty raised his voice. "I must say I did not find it humorous, and I am not at all sure Alice did either."

Dodgson had a sudden urge to leave the room and run down the stairs, but he was overcome with the strange feeling that would be rude. He had guests.

The dodo swooped through the room, narrowly missing Dodgson's head.

"I did not think you were able to fly," Dodgson said. He tried to comb down his hair with his hands.

"Shows how much you know," the dodo said, his plumage an iridescent blue.

"Am I correct in assuming that you do not exist?" Dodgson asked politely.

"You are correct in nothing," the bird said, flying off.

He felt boundaries between species dissolving: skeletons changing shape. Bones stretching and shrinking. Ape becomes man. Man becomes bird.

Humpty said: "I can't imagine why she endured it for so long, her head striking against a roof, being beaten violently in the face by a pigeon, nearly having her head cut off with an ax."

"Poor thing," said the Hatter.

Dodgson covered his ears but he could still hear the voices.

"Opera, theater, hunting, wine, actresses, prostitutes, opium dens, gambling, races, Darwin, inversion, atheism, gluttony, adultery, lustful imaginings," the Hatter rattled off wearily.

But Dodgson only stared at him miserably.

"Undo, redo, I understand it entirely, I am quite familiar

with the tendency," the Hatter said in a more conciliatory tone. "We all have an arbitrary execution hanging over our heads, don't we? Off with your head." He smiled and made a throat-cutting gesture with his hand.

Dodgson stepped back. "I do not want."

Humpty taunted: *"We are but older children, dear. Who fret to find our bedtime near."*

"You look bewildered," he continued. "Turn yourself inside out."

"You fall into a grave and you don't die," said the Hatter.

"Self spelled backward is flesh," said Humpty.

"Almost."

"No one sees the autobiographical strand."

"Confessions of St. Augustine by Lewis Carroll."

"The sins and salvations."

Dodgson saw it—this museum of his feelings laid out in front of him.

He was standing with Alice in his room.

He wanted to cup her face in his hands.

He wanted to live forever—

It was the end of the world. As in medieval maps where the land ends abruptly and the blue of the sea is dotted with dragons.

His room was crowded with his intentions, shaking and nodding and chattering. He wanted to run away, but that was out of the question. Even standing was out of the question.

How to tell the story without telling the story? To stutter the sentence so badly no one would understand what he was saying.

The funny thing was that beneath the shimmer of the drug

he was thinking with logical precision, like a proof writing itself out on the blackboard.

Dodgson swigged the laudanum.

Drink me.

His body understood, as if it was written into every cell and particle, that it could not withstand any more of the drug. He tilted the bottle further.

"Out like a candle," Humpty said, smiling sweetly.

Dodgson heard a rapping, a rapping so insistent, so different from the rest of the noises, woody and hollower, that he realized finally someone might be outside. The door swung open and there was Hunt.

"I only wanted—" Dodgson started to explain.

But he realized the words were not coming out of his mouth. He was too tired, but tired was the wrong word, because his mind was perfectly clear, each thought sharp and glistening. The laudanum had spilled on his trousers and down his chest, soaking him fuchsia, a flower-shaped stain on his shirt. Hunt was on the floor, holding him like a child. He had taken the nearly empty bottle out of his hands.

What is the worst that could happen? Hunt had once said. And the phrase caught in his mind. What is the worst that could happen? Imagine it happening, and then imagine that you are still standing, like a soldier on a field, the one upright surviving thing.

"You will be fine." He could hear Hunt's voice. "You will be fine."

Dodgson suddenly felt fine, with his head resting against Hunt's chest . . . back to his own childhood, when he was still in skirts, his hair in chestnut ringlets, in the garden with his sisters, his mother inside the lace curtain, at the window, embroidering. Surrounded by the girls and the strong sweet smell of daffodils, in the tall grasses, the girls all around him, pressing into him. *Charlie Darling.*

The picture came at him again. Himself submerged in their skirts, outnumbered and overpowered and lost. They looked so similar, his sisters, plain, snub-nosed, dark-haired. Himself almost smothering, there in their skirts, an uncomfortable rumpled boychild trying to breathe.

You don't exist, Alice. He dreamt Alice up. And that was the strange thing, as he became light-headed, the air in the room thinner, as he saw through the slits of his eyes, the room moving and vibrating in the most peculiar way: He realized there was no Alice.

20

Mrs. Liddell showed Hunt into one of the more formal rooms they had added onto the deanery. She wore a shiny dark blue dress with lace trim. Her hair was pulled back tightly, leaving her face oddly vulnerable and exposed.

The room was too grand for the three of them, but Mrs. Liddell wanted the official distance of the room, the treaty-signing aspect. She wanted to surround herself with the vague presences of tradition, the frowning portraits of former deans.

Meanwhile, the living dean was sitting in a leather chair by the back window with the mildly dazed expression of someone who had just looked up from a book, an expression that, considering he was a scholar, he almost never had in normal life.

"I think you will understand my position in this matter," Mrs. Liddell said quietly. "He should not be living next to decent families."

"I understand perfectly," Hunt said. He was sitting on an uncomfortable wood-framed settee, with a large globe at his elbow.

"Her father can barely look at her," she said.

"I understand," he said, glancing at the dean.

The conversation they were not having stirred beneath the surface, trilled through the air, the possibility that none of them raised. That Mr. Dodgson had done more than take Alice's picture. The languor of the photographs could not fail to draw him in. And hadn't he shown himself as a man utterly without morals? What if, after he had put down the camera, he had gone to help her put her clothes back on. . . . It was too awful to develop the scenario. To let the images reproduce as in a darkroom. But they would never know. They would never allow themselves to utter out loud the possibility, because of what it would mean to Alice's future, because of how unthinkable it was. And yet they thought it. Each one of them thought it as they sat there with the sunset pouring through the large panes of the window, bleaching the oriental rug pale peach. They thought of nothing else.

"And can you imagine," said Mrs. Liddell, "stealing into our garden in the middle of the night?"

"Perhaps he came to voice his regrets," Hunt said. This possibility sounded absurd even to him.

"In the middle of the night?"

"These past few days have been extremely hard on everyone," Hunt continued.

"How could the church allow him to get this far?" Mrs. Liddell asked. "The *Reverend* C. L. Dodgson? And then of course there is the matter of his mathematical contribution.

What has he ever produced? What has he truly added to the field?"

The dean maintained his air of scholarly absorption.

Hunt said nothing. What Mr. Dodgson had contributed to the field of mathematics hardly seemed the point. But Mrs. Liddell was looking at him expectantly.

Hunt felt the delicacy of his position. Mrs. Liddell had called him when she discovered the photographs, because she knew that he had treated Dodgson, the way one might call a lion tamer when the lion has escaped from the circus. She thought he might know Dodgson's habits, might be able to clarify the situation. Which for some reason was at once entirely obvious and entirely obscure. She seemed to want to be told what to feel. And when she discovered how easily and gently he heard her concerns about Alice, she decided that she wanted him for herself. She wanted to throw herself into his care. She wanted to take him over. And now he had become the emissary of Mr. Dodgson.

Though he only half admitted it to himself, Hunt had hoped to get a glimpse of Alice. But she was upstairs in her bedroom reading *Robinson Crusoe*.

The dean poured himself a brandy and water from the crystal decanters on the table. He nodded toward Hunt. Hunt demurred.

"Of course, you are entirely justified in your feelings." Hunt paused. "But I believe it is in the best interest of your daughter and the university as a whole for the unfortunate business to remain quiet."

Mrs. Liddell stared at him. In the dark room, her eyes seemed as enormous and black as Alice's.

"As far as I am concerned it was a slightly bohemian

project gone awry," Hunt continued. "And there is no call for any of us to make anything more of it."

Mrs. Liddell wrapped both hands around her teacup.

"A slightly bohemian project?" she repeated slowly. "And who is our mathematical hero then, Lord Byron?"

But she heard the bargain. She realized that if Dodgson were run out of Oxford, as she ardently wished him to be, then Alice would in effect be run out as well. If nothing else, Dodgson had achieved a sort of subterranean marriage of their destinies: what happened to him would also happen, in one way or another, to Alice. And Mrs. Liddell could not take that risk. Even if it meant living next door to this depraved individual for the rest of her life and smiling at him at large breakfasts and dinners. Alice had to be protected.

For a second Hunt thought he saw a white ruffle move behind the curtain.

"I suppose it's decided. We shall simply let it be," Mrs. Liddell said finally.

"It's settled then," the dean said, rising slowly from his chair. "And now if you'll excuse me, Dr. Hunt, I have pressing business I must return to."

Edith was hidden behind the curtain, hot behind the heavy fabric. She could not believe what was happening. She stood there miserably, unable to move, breathing damask. She could feel the photographs receding as in a dream. Fairly soon, they will never have existed.

Dodgson was leaving for a few weeks at the seaside. At Hunt's urging, he had decided that he would gather his manuscripts and leave Oxford for a while. And so to his great surprise he found himself engrossed in the highly optimistic task of packing: he was sorting through his clothes and choosing which books to bring along with him (Aristotle not Euclid, *Antony and Cleopatra* not *A Midsummer Night's Dream*). He wrapped his shirts and gloves carefully in tissue and placed each bundle into the open suitcase on his bed.

He checked himself in the mirror. He was never very good at endings. Even in his writing. His favored exit, his easy way out was always "it was just a dream." But what about when it wasn't just a dream?

What if she had died? His mind circled the thought like a flock of vultures. Tenniel's wife Julia had died of tuberculosis shortly after they were married. And he could see the artist's unhappiness in the knitted eyebrows and drooping eyes of his drawings. Rossetti's wife, Lizzie, had died of an overdose of laudanum, and of his infidelities, or so people surmised, which manifested itself as what in Rossetti's life? An extra glass of claret at dinner, maybe. Excessive bursts of frenetic late night conversation on the subject of free verse?

He felt a tightening in his chest. He couldn't allow himself to think this way. But he had written the part for her himself. *It might end in my going out like a candle. And she tried to fancy what the flame of a candle looks like after the candle is blown out, for she could not remember ever having seen such a thing.* He tried to stop the thoughts looping through his mind. Her dying would have been easier; the sorrow waterfalling through his chest, the right sorrow.

But she would live. The idea came to him of Alice's life sprawled out like the university, complicated towers and court-yards, curving paths and spires, libraries, arches, pockets of green, without him in it.

He was waiting for generosity to flow, for the moment where he released her to happiness. Let her go and be happy. Only it didn't come.

Instead he was caught in the dream in which you are late to somewhere you desperately need to be but cannot get to. Her life continuing blithely on. Each minute blotting him out: if she exists without him then he does not.

He closed the suitcase and lifted it. Heavy but not too.

He could no longer think of her whole, could think of her only partially, as through the crack of an open door: the arched eyebrows, the slightly upturned nose, the gap between her front teeth when she smiled.

The paradox: how do you lose something you never had?

The answer: There was another way to have. A transparent stretch of space between you. To love from a distance, through that space, more deeply, more colorfully, so it can be seen from faraway like a flag. Eventually the space itself fills you. The air entering your body and replacing your blood, running through you. The half-pleasant feeling of not being there.

He was going to Sandown, Isle of Wight. A small, clean room with a balcony. He thought of how the seaside might work. The quieting roar of the ocean. The salty wet air against his face. He never went into the water. But he would walk, trousers rolled, feet in the sand, passing ladies with parasols, men in straw boaters, gulls swooping through clear blue.

He thought of the bat flying out the window, and her looking up at him like he, suddenly omnipotent and Greek godlike, had orchestrated the whole thing, the bat, tray, servant, sandwiches, everything. *Twinkle, twinkle, little bat, how I wonder what you're at. Up above the world you fly, like a tea-tray in the sky.*

Of course the sadness, the looking back, was there all along. There was always all along this poignance. This sense of threat built into the sweetness, hunkered down in it.

He folded a copy of *Cornhill Magazine,* and put it into the side pocket of his battered black suitcase for the train.

From the moment he met her, Dodgson had been afraid that his friendship with her would fall violently apart. But in the fear was a wish, a wish to relieve the pressure the situation placed on him. What if it didn't end. What if she grew so large she. What if.

The idea of being alone was not without solace. He was tired of all the subterranean strife. There was a shameful or sensible part of him that rejoiced. It was over.

Alice was squatting on the floor in front of her doll's house, not sure whether to put the striped sofa in the parlor or the sitting room. The sitting room was more comfortable, but the parlor was grander, more suitable for company. The cat rubbed against the corner of the house, her fur blotting out the sky. Alice looked at the drapes, which were rose damask, made from the same cloth as the curtains downstairs but a little faded, and thought to herself that it was time to replace them. Suddenly it occurred to her that the cake was about to burn. She moved the little Alice down to the kitchen to save it. A perfect pink cake. Not even singed. The little Alice set it carefully down on the table. The baby cried in the bedroom. The little Alice ran up the stairs and picked up the baby from the cradle. The nurse was sitting there in the rocking chair in the corner doing nothing. The little Alice carried the baby down to the cake.

It was the baby's birthday. There was a knock on the door. It was Charles.

❦

Dodgson sat on the train, watching the countryside pass by in a blur, steel sky, brick houses, wild, cragged brush. This stretch of England all looked the same to him. *A slow sort of country! said the queen. Now here, you see it takes all the running you can do, to keep in the same place.* The motion of the train rocked him as he tried to sip his cold tea. A small, curly-haired girl of around five passed through the corridor. He looked at her. She smiled at him, a large toothy smile, with dimples. He put his tea down and shook out his morning paper. Later, she passed by again. She had a round face and milky skin. Her hair was amazing, a wild soft mass of reds, blonds, and browns. He reached into the suitcase and took out the bat and three puzzles he had stuffed at the bottom at the last minute and laid them out on the empty seat next to him. She stood shyly in the corridor, half hidden by the doorway to the compartment. Her enormous tawny eyes were fixed on the bat. He held it up to her, and she went over to touch its face. He dusted it off with his handkerchief, and wound it up carefully. It trembled in the palm of his hand and lifting its wings, it flew.

A boat, beneath a sunny sky
Lingering onward dreamily
In an evening of July—

Children three that nestle near,
Eager eye and willing ear,
Pleased a simple tale to hear—

Long has paled that sunny sky:
Echoes fade and memories die:
Autumn frosts have slain July.

Still she haunts me, phantomwise.
Alice moving under skies
Never seen by waking eyes.

Children yet, the tale to hear,
Eager eye and willing ear,
Lovingly shall nestle near.

In a Wonderland they lie,
Dreaming as the days go by,
Dreaming as the summers die:

Ever drifting down the stream—
Lingering in the golden gleam—
Life, what is it but a dream?

—Lewis Carroll
from *Through the Looking Glass*

AUTHOR'S NOTE

This book is a work of fiction inspired by the life of Charles Dodgson and his relationship with Alice Liddell. I have altered geography, chronology, and history where it served the purposes of the novel. The letters quoted in this book, with the exception of those on pages 94 and 193, are real. The manuscript of the ballad opera and the note on page 184 are drawn from the unpublished manuscripts of Lewis Carroll in the Berol Collection at the Fales Library, New York University. The diary entries are invented.

There was a significant rift between the Liddell family and Charles Dodgson, beginning in the last days of June 1863. Before this, Dodgson was a frequent guest at the deanery. For five months afterward his diary offers no mention of the Liddells until he ran into them at a Christ Church theatrical and wrote: "But I held aloof from them as I have done all this term." His contact with the family in subsequent years was intermittent and formal. Biographers and historians have never isolated the cause of this break to their satisfaction, though many have speculated that it must have had something to do with Dodgson's relationship with Alice, who was then eleven. In her eighties Alice Liddell Hargreaves wrote a sunny reminiscence of her relationship with Lewis Carroll in *Cornhill Magazine*. One line leaps out of the dreamy prose: "Unfortunately my mother tore up all the letters that Mr. Dodgson wrote to me when I was a small girl." But Alice never elaborated. The portions of Dodgson's diaries that might have explained what happened were destroyed.

Charles Dodgson visited a speech therapist in Hastings named Dr. James Hunt, who was the author of *Stammering and Stuttering: Their Nature and Treatment* (1861). Hunt was also honorary secretary of the Ethnological Society, but after alienating many of its members with his free speculation on man's origins, he founded the Anthropological Society in 1863.

In my research I have been helped by many more books than I can name, but the following extraordinary works stand out: Lewis Carroll's complete works; Charles Dodgson's *Euclid and His Modern Rivals* and other mathematical texts; Morton Cohen's biography, *Lewis Carroll* and *Reflections in a Looking Glass*; Tim Hilton's Ruskin biography, both volumes; Derek Hudson's *Munby: Man of Two Worlds* and *Lewis Carroll*; Martin Gardner's *The Annotated Alice*; Anne Clark's *The Real Alice*; Helmut Gernsheim's *Lewis Carroll, Photographer*; George MacDonald's *The Light Princess*; and Ruskin's *Praeterita*, as well as critical essays by Virginia Woolf, W. H. Auden, Vladimir Nabokov, and Edmund Wilson; the poems of

Christina Rossetti, William Wordsworth, and Andrew Marvell; and the novels of Anthony Trollope.

I am also greatly indebted to Langford Reed's *The Life of Lewis Carroll*, Stuart Dodgson Collingwood's *The Life and Letters of Lewis Carroll*, Roger Lancelyn Green's *The Story of Lewis Carroll* and *The Diaries of Lewis Carroll*, Morton Cohen's *The Letters of Lewis Carroll*, John Pudney's *Lewis Carroll and His World*, and to Uli Knoepflmacher's *Adventures in Childland* and *Forbidden Journeys* and James Kincaid's *Childloving: The Erotic Child and Victorian Culture*. Also helpful were Rodney Engen's *Sir John Tenniel: Alice's White Knight*; Roger Simpson's *Sir John Tenniel: Aspects of His Work*; the Rev. Henry Thompson's *Henry George Liddell and Christ Church*; Frances Thomas's *Christina Rossetti*; the memoirs written by women who knew Charles Dodgson when they were children, including those of Isa Bowman, Beatrice Hatch, and Alice herself; E.G.W. Bill and J.F.A Mason's *Christ Church and Reform*; James Morris's *Oxford*; Hugh de Selincourt's *Oxford from Within*; W. E. Sherwood's *Oxford Yesterday*; *The Oxford Book of Oxford* edited by Jan Morris; Virginia Berridge's *Opium and the People*; Steven Marcus's *The Other Victorians*; Margaret Dalziel's *Popular Fiction a Hundred Years Ago*; Theodore Hook's *The Widow and the Marquess*; Warren Weaver's "Mathematical Manuscripts of Lewis Carroll"; Graham Ovenden's *Pre-Raphaelite Photography*; Elizabeth Prettejohn's *The Art of the Pre-Raphaelites*; W.H.D. Rouse's *A History of Rugby School*; and Thomas De Quincey's *Confessions of an English Opium-Eater*.

My deepest thanks to Susan Kamil and Suzanne Gluck for

their energy and faith. To Richard Lamb, Alan Isler, and Richard Kaye for reading early drafts. To Emily Carter Roiphe, Theodore Jacobs, David Samuels, Larissa Macfarquhar, Deb Kogan, Linda Rattner, Jon Jon Goulian, Elyse Cheney, Sloan Harris, and Karen Gerwin for their encouragement, distraction, and other help. To Uli Knoepflmacher for his Victorian literature class at Princeton, and to the Fales Library at New York University and the trustees of the C. L. Dodgson estate for their kind permission to quote from several of Dodgson's unpublished letters and manuscripts. To Anne, Herman, and Becky Roiphe for their endless patience and opinions and support. And to Harry Chernoff for everything.

ABOUT THE AUTHOR

KATIE ROIPHE received her Ph.D. from Princeton in English literature. Her articles have appeared in *The New York Times, The Washington Post, Esquire, Harper's,* and *The New Yorker,* among many others. Her previous books are *The Morning After* and *Last Night in Paradise.* She lives in New York City.